Terror Isla

By

Lynda L. Lock

&

Dedication – Paradise Lost

Lawrie Lock; March 3rd 1942 – September 3rd 2018

Paradise is normally considered to be a place, but for me paradise is a person; my husband, adventure partner, world-traveler, lover and best friend - Lawrie Lock.

This is the one-year anniversary of his passing and in celebration of his wonderfully wacky life I am dedicating this newest novel to son John Lock and his beautiful family; Maia, Caitlin, Ethan and Evan. They are my sunlight in this storm of grief.

Lawrie's genes and his spirit of adventure lives on in the following generations.

Handsome dudes: Evan, John, Ethan.

Pretty ladies: Maia, Caitlin.

Chapter 1

April 1st Cancun

Sweat trickled down his back and his gut cramped as he weakly grinned at the security camera. He heard the thick outer door hydraulically close, isolating him from the bank's customers. He would remain locked in the tiny air-conditioned space while an electronic timer ticked off the minutes. Then the inner door would open giving him free access to the secure areas of the bank.

He inhaled and held his breath a moment then slowly let it leak out of his lungs. *Just stay calm. It would be okay. Just keep thinking about how much they are paying you.*

Three days ago, as he was leaving another branch of the same bank, two lean muscular men had flanked him. Each man had clamped a powerful hand on his skinny forearms, efficiently trapping him between their hard bodies.

"Be quiet. I have a gun." The taller one had growled with a strong Eastern European accent.

Russian? Romanian? Ukrainian? The technician had no idea. He was just shit-scared.

"You're coming with us." The other man pulled his tool satchel from his hand. Dacey's feet barely made contact with the sidewalk as his captors rushed him to a plain white delivery van, slid the side door open and hustled him inside. The van sped away as a dark smelly hood was dropped over his head, and his hands were secured behind his back. At that point he pissed himself.

A short confusing ride later and he was dragged from the van, half carried into a building then shoved into an elevator. Two or three floors later, they pulled him out and dumped him onto a wooden chair and secured him, leaving the covering on his head.

He wasn't sure if he was on the second or third floor because he was too frightened to count the number of pings the elevator made as they moved upwards. His captors had not said another thing after grabbing him. He had wanted to say, *please don't hurt me. I will do whatever you say,* instead unable to speak he had silently wept.

"Dacey Uicab. A pleasure to meet you." A deep masculine voice said.

"How do you know my name?" Dacey whimpered. His mind raced with scenarios, none of which made any sense. Sure, he'd had sex a couple of times with his sister-in-law, but that wasn't a big deal. They had both enjoyed it. He had also lied on how many hours he worked for his employer, but who didn't fudge their hours a little?

"Who are you?" He timidly asked.

"You do not need to know who I am," The person replied.

"What do you want with me? I haven't done anything wrong," Dacey whined. He hated physical confrontation of any type. As a schoolboy he had been terrorized by the bigger, stronger bullies. He had always been a small, geeky guy. A sweaty timid nerd.

"We are just having a little chat," The voice said. Dacey bobbed his head in submissive agreement. It was a difficult maneuver because of the heavy, stinky hood but he wanted to convince the man he was cooperative.

"I have a business proposition for you." Now the man sounded positively avuncular.

"A business proposition, that sounds interesting." Dacey's pulse changed from fast and spiky to a tiny bit slower and smoother. Maybe they weren't going to hurt him after all. He concentrated on listening. The space sounded echoey and empty, like a warehouse without much stock.

"You work for the company that does maintenance for various bank ATMs."

"Si?" He replied, his pulse returned to its erratic rhythm. He longed to wipe the stinging sweat out of his eyes but his hands were tightly bound with what felt like plastic straps. *Breathe. Just keep breathing, in and out. Calm down and think.*

"You have a wife, two very young children, plus parents, five siblings, aunties, uncles and lots of cousins."

Darcy silently nodded and felt more warm urine leaking down his leg. They had been investigating his life. *Why?*

"Bueno! I have the right man." The man sharply slapped his hands together, causing Dacey to reflexively jerk. "I have a new generation of Bluetooth transmitters that I want installed inside the ATMs that you service."

"Why me?" He bleated. Even to his own ears he sounded like a loser.

"Why not you?"

Dacey didn't respond. He was too frightened to think of a logical answer.

"Besides if you agree to my terms I pay very well," Said the disembodied voice.

"What are your ... terms?" Dacey squeaked out. The rank smell of his fear filled his nostrils.

"Follow orders and don't ask questions."

"What happens if I can't accept your terms?"

"You'll die."

Dacey gasped. "I ... accept. Please ... don't kill me."

"Good. Emanoil, give Dacey a rundown on how the skimmers work." A chair scrapped against a hard floor, "I have another appointment," He said in a cheerfully breezy tone.

To Dacey's ears, right at that moment the man sounded like a regular guy, like an important and busy executive rather than a stone-cold killer.

"Yes, of course boss," The man named Emanoil replied, saying a word that sounded like boss, but with a different twist to the pronunciation.

Dacey heard a door shut, and then the rough hood was jerked off of his head. He blinked; bright sunlight streamed through large windows. He was in an empty office building, not a warehouse. Free from the hot headgear he gulped in the cooler air, and smelled the humiliating stink of his fear and piss.

"Welcome to our little family," Emanoil sneered, as he released Dacey's arms. "I am Emanoil and this is Ionut. You don't need to know our last names."

"Mucho gusto," Dacey replied automatically. He rubbed his bruised wrists as his nervous glances ping-ponged between his captors. They were so similar in appearance they could be brothers or cousins. Both men were lean, taller than him, with dark hair buzzed close to their pale skin and short beards. Ionut's straight, sharp nose and deep-set dark eyes gave him the fierce appearance of an eagle, zeroing in on his prey. Emanoil looked like a skinny but powerful bear, muscles bunched and ready to attack.

"What now?"

"We show you how the devices work and you install them in the ATMs," Ionut replied. His cold leer settled on Dacey's face.

Dacey was certain this was how a mouse felt when it realized that a predator had seen it. Exposed. About to die. His heart hammered faster.

"Walk." Emanoil rammed his arm into Dacey's back causing him to lurch forward a step or two.

"Okay, okay. Please don't hurt me," Dacey said as he scrambled to stay ahead of Emanoil. In a momentary spurt of bravery, he asked, "How ... how much will I be paid?"

"If you do a good job, you can earn up to one hundred times your wages working for the boss."

"Seriously? A hundred times my wages," Dacey sputtered, momentarily losing his concentration he stumbled and nearly tripped. *Maybe this wasn't so bad after all.*

"Yes, but the trick is to live long enough to spend it," Emanoil replied, his mocking voice whispered close to Dacey's ear.

Chapter 2

April 2nd Isla Mujeres

"Damn it! What do you mean not authorized?" Jessica Sanderson cursed the ATM. She could see her reflection in the screen; blonde-haired, blue-eyed, lightly tanned with an annoyed expression creasing her face. A small slice of the artwork that started on her left shoulder and continued to her wrist was also visible. The realistic face of a sea turtle peered inquisitively at the ATM.

"Problems, Jess?"

Jessica turned her head and grimaced over her shoulder at her friend Yasmin Medina de Mendoza. Yassy was standing nearby but not close enough to intrude on her privacy. Even without her ever-present stiletto heels, Yasmin was slightly taller that Jess. Her mass of shoulder length, dark curly hair was shot through with blonde highlights. Her green eyes were attention-grabbing.

"This dumbass machine must be broken. I'll try another one," Jessica said stepping across to the second ATM in the alcove. Pushing her card inside the slot, she followed the prompts on the screen, then got the same message. "What the hell?"

"Maybe your card has been compromised?" Suggested Yasmin.

She spun fully around, "You think so?"

"There's warnings all over Facebook about ATMs being compromised on a regular basis," Yasmin said, with a little shrug of one shoulder. "Maybe you should go in the bank and check on your account."

"Are you going to try this one?" Jessica pointed at the device. "Maybe it's the machine and not my card."

"No, I'll go inside and get my cash from the tellers. Just in case."

Jessica opened the door to the bank and looked at the long line of people patiently waiting for one of the two tellers that were open for business. She checked the time on her phone, and shook her head as she let the door shut again. "I'll do it first thing tomorrow morning when the bank opens at nine. I don't want to wait. I have a lunch date with Maricruz in a few minutes."

Yasmin laughed, "Jess, it's Mexico. It won't matter if you are a few minutes or twenty minutes late."

"I'm Canadian. I have a national obligation to be on time," Jessica retorted with a cheeky smile.

"If you need some money, I have a little bit," Yasmin offered, as she reached inside her shoulder bag and took out a two hundred peso note. "This is all I have, but you are welcome to it."

Jessica pulled a tiny cloth purse out of her left pocket, undid the zipper and thumbed through the bills inside. "No thanks, Yassy. I'm okay for lunch but that's about all. I'll take care of this tomorrow."

"Okay, if you are sure," Yasmin replied, then added, "Where's Sparky?" She asked referring to Jessica's short-legged, rescue-mutt.

"He's waiting in *Frita Bandita,* my golf cart," She replied. Eighteen months ago, when she found him hiding in the bushes, he was skinny, dirty, tick infested and terrified of people. Now he was a confident happy dog who loved going for rides on or in anything that moved; a cart, moto, car or boat it didn't matter as long as it was moving.

"Is he going to lunch with you?"

Jessica smiled slyly, "Of course, I only go to the restaurants that allow my famous pooch to lie under the table."

Yasmin laughed, "Okay, say hi to Maricruz for me."

"Why don't you join us?"

"Thanks, but I have plans with my honey," She replied. "He said he wants to discuss something with me."

"Okay, give Carlos a hug from me. I'll see you at work tomorrow.

~

"Yes! A parking spot," Jessica said. Wheeling the light vehicle across the pavement and onto a sandy strip of land next to the restaurant entrance she shut off the engine. Isla Mujeres was one of a handful of places in Mexico where it was legal to drive a golf cart on public streets. She loved the freedom of owning a vehicle, basic as it was. It had a one-cylinder motor, seats front and back, four tires and rims, a steering wheel, headlights and a plastic windshield that could be raised to keep rain out of the driver's eyes during the frequent and short tropical downpours. Her arms were the turn signals.

She turned off the ignition key and unclipped Sparky's leash. When he wanted to sit on the seat beside her, she looped the lead around the back of the seat and clipped to his harness. If he was in the mood to stand on the floor and lean into the cooling breeze, she tied his leash around the steering column. Anything to keep him from tumbling out of the cart on the corners. In the past he had fallen out twice, scaring her half to death with the thought that she could have run over her own dog. She refastened his lead to the harness and stepped onto the sand.

"Okay bud, let's go see if Maricruz is here yet." Sparky's fuzzy eyebrows danced above his expressive eyes.

Tucked in behind the Pemex gas station in Centro, the restaurant had excellent food, great drinks, and it was her favourite location to watch the fishermen working on their boats, or catch the evening sunset. Her good friends Diego Avalos and Pedro Velazquez frequently docked their fifty-eight-foot Viking sport fishing boat the *Bruja del Mar* at the wharf when they had fishing and photography charters booked. Today's weather was warm with a slight breeze and they would probably be out with a group.

Several of the waiters waved a greeting and one pointed at her favourite table, on the far corner overlooking the ocean. Maricruz was already seated with a glass of red wine in front of her, a closed menu rested beside her hand.

Maricruz spotted Jessica and Sparky and lifted her glass of wine in greeting. Jessica nodded and pointed at herself. "Me too please." She said as the waiter looked her way.

"Claro," He replied, indicating that he understood.

"Hola Maricruz," Jessica dipped her head to give her friend a kiss on the cheek. "Cómo estás? Normally geared-up and armed, the beautiful raven-haired woman, Teniente Maricruz Zapata, was a tough and capable lieutenant in the Mexican Navy. Today she was dressed much like Jessica in shorts, a cute t-shirt and sparkly sandals, the difference being, her handmade leather purse probably held a nine-millimeter handgun.

"Bien, bien, y tu?" Maricruz replied.

"Todo bien. I don't see the *Bruja*. Are the guys out on a charter?" Shortly after Hurricane Pablo had battered their peaceful island the previous August, Maricruz had started dating Pedro Velazquez.

"Si, they have a group who want to photograph sailfish."

"Good, those clients pay very well," She said as she tied the leash to her chair. He wouldn't normally wander off, but occasionally his famous sense of smell would lead him astray, or more correctly would lead her straight into another *Sparky situation* as Diego liked to tease. Sparky had helped Yasmin and Jessica locate a pirate's secret stash, rescued Carlos from a killer, located a missing but very dead islander, and more recently saved Jessica and her Auntie Pattie from a cartel assassin. A few of her friends had taken to calling her stocky, mix-breed pooch *The Sparkinator* because of his heroic antics.

"Anything new?" Jessica asked. She nodded her thanks as the waiter set her glass of wine beside her.

"Not much. How about with you?"

"Auntie Pattie is slowly improving. She has started rehab for the gunshot wound in her shoulder."

"That's very good news," Maricruz said, "By the way, I am curious. I haven't seen you and Luis together recently. Everything okay?"

Jessica waggled her hand back and forth, "More or less, I guess."

"Any particular reason?"

"No, not really," Jessica replied, "We just seemed to have drifted apart."

"Maybe it just wasn't meant to be," Maricruz replied.

Jessica shrugged. She really had no clear idea why, but she definitely had lost interest in Luis. "Any more information on the Cuban girls? It's been almost six weeks since they escaped the traffickers," She said, steering the conversation in another direction.

Maricruz stared pensively into her wine glass, then she raised her eyes. "They are still being detained. We've been told they have to be returned to Cuba. We're just not sure when."

"Those poor kids," Jessica said. "Their families thought they were being hired by American families as nannies and housekeepers."

"I know, and most of their families won't be happy to have them back. They are just another mouth to feed," Maricruz agreed. "But our hands are tied by an agreement put in place in 2008 between the USA and Mexico."

"What changed?"

"Before 2008 Cubans caught entering Mexico illegally were rarely sent back. Most were held for a short period, then released and told to report for their court hearing in two weeks. They didn't of course, but would continue moving north to Texas. Once they reached the American border, they could present their documents and claim political refugee status."

"Well, the good thing is we rescued them from being forced into the sex-trade by the cartel and other gangs."

"For now," Maricruz sceptically amended.

Chapter 3

April 2nd Isla Mujeres

Yasmin tucked her withdrawal into her purse as she walked out of the bank and headed towards Hidalgo Avenue. Four years ago, she had started working for Carlos Mendoza as a waitress at the *Loco Lobo Restaurante*. Jessica had hired on the following year and the two women immediately bonded, becoming close friends.

When Jessica first moved to the island, she was unsure how long she would stay in the tiny community so she was content to remain a server. Yasmin on the other hand wanted more responsibility. She had rapidly been promoted to be the evening bar-tender, and more recently the assistant manager of the popular restaurant. She was efficient and organized with the added benefit of being fluent in Spanish and English, plus a few phrases of Mayan. Attracted to Carlos she hadn't pushed the relationship, just letting it develop slowly as they became close friends and then lovers.

Since their marriage on February 22nd Carlos had transferred the title of the business and his house into both of their names. He said he wanted her to feel that she was truly his partner in all things; life, love and adventures. He had assured her that his long-ago first marriage was truly a thing of the past, despite his ex-wife Elena Hernandez unexpectedly entering his house a few years later. Carlos hadn't realized that Elena still had a door key. He had immediately contacted a locksmith and changed all the locks.

Then one evening after a couple of glasses of wine Carlos had self-consciously confided to Yasmin that he been reluctant to ask her out because he was nine years older. His wilder youth behind him, he had grown into a successful businessman and he was worried she might think he was too staid and boring.

Far from it, she had reassured him with a long and passionate kiss. The age difference had never entered her mind because what she saw was a sexy man with a wacky sense of humour and a kind heart. She could get lost in his chocolate brown eyes when he held her close. She loved to kiss the end of her finger and then trace the faint scar on his face, as if she could erase the mark. It ran from his left eyebrow to the tip of his mouth; the reminder of a youthful indiscretion. Whether they were dancing, making love, or just hanging out together their life was pure bliss.

Arriving at the restaurant Yasmin headed towards his tiny office at the rear of the building. She sauntered towards his open door purposely putting a bit of sass into her walk. She smiled when, as he called it, his internal radar pinged. He instinctively knew she was nearby.

Carlos leaned back in his chair with his hands laced behind his head, and grinned appreciatively at her cat-walk strut. "Buenas tardes Señora Mendoza," he said, standing to kiss her.

"Y, muy buenas tardes a ti, Señor Mendoza." She responded when they unglued their lips.

"Where would you like to have lunch?" He asked. "I need to get out for a bit to clear my head."

"Jessica and Maricruz are at Bally Hoo. We could join them." She settled herself in a chair and crossed her legs, purposely showing a bit of toned thigh.

"Are you trying to seduce me woman?" He bounced his eyebrows appreciatively.

"Perhaps." She pursed her lips into a movie-star moue.

"Save that thought," He said. "Right now, I have an idea I want to discuss privately with you so, no, I don't want to join the ladies at Bally Hoo."

She considered for a moment, "Then how about the fish market on the beach?"

"Sure, it's expensive and away from Centro so we won't bump into a lot of acquaintances there."

"We could go someplace else less expensive, if you want."

"No, it's perfect. There won't be many islanders, mostly people from Cancun."

"Are we taking my moto?" She asked.

"A taxi would be better, then we can share a bottle of wine and relax."

"Worried about road-side Breathalyzer checks, are you?" Yasmin quipped. On the island the road-side sobriety checks could, on the rare occasion, be an actual Breathalyzer reusing a plastic straw-shaped sample collector that had been used for all of the previous customers. Or sometimes the detainee might be asked to blow into the cupped hands of a policía constable. The constable would then sniff their own hands to check for the scent of alcohol. But it was really about money as much as it was about getting the drunks off the road. Deep pockets could buy forgiveness.

Carlos smiled, "Not really, but why take the chance?"

A few minutes later a taxi dropped them off at the oceanfront restaurant a short distance south of Playa Lancheros. Holding hands Carlos and Yasmin walked towards the covered deck.

"Do you have a table for two with a good view?" Carlos asked the waiter.

"Of course, Carlos," The man replied with a welcoming smile.

"I'm sorry, I don't remember your name," Carlos replied.

"*No hay problema*, we only met briefly once. *Mi nombre es Paco*."

"Mucho gusto." Carlos shook hands with Paco.

Pulling out a chair Paco addressed Yasmin, "Do you like this table Señora Mendoza?"

"Si, gracias Paco, and please my name is Yasmin. Calling me Señora Mendoza makes me feel old," She said with a warm smile as she sat down.

"As you wish."

"We aren't in a rush, so please just bring us a nice bottle of red wine to share, and we will order later," Carlos said.

Yasmin reached across to hold hands with Carlos, "So, what is this big secret you want to discuss with me?"

"Secret?" He said, feigning surprise, "I just wanted to sneak away for lunch with a beautiful woman." He furtively glanced over his shoulder. "Please don't tell my wife. She is very possessive."

Yasmin laughed and he leaned in for a smooch. "Damn it, Carlos, tell me," She demanded.

"Okay, I give up," He raised her hand and gently kissed her fingers. "You mentioned after *Hurricane Pablo* you wanted to remodel or at least redecorate the *Loco Lobo*, but I have another idea."

"And?" Yasmin said, rolling her hand in a *keep talking* motion.

Paco returned at that moment with a bottle of wine, held label out, "Will this suit you?" He asked showing the label first to Carlos then to Yasmin.

"Si, that's perfect," Carlos replied, glancing at the name on the bottle, "We don't need to sample it, gracias. I'm familiar with the brand."

Yasmin lightly drummed her fingers on the table top while Paco poured a glass for her, and then one for Carlos.

"Any appetizers to start?"

Carlos glanced at Yasmin, "Would you like to share a couple of starters with the wine?"

She rolled her eyes at him, "Yes of course, whatever you want to order is fine with me."

His eyes creased with laughter when he saw her exasperated expression.

Paco noted their orders and once he was safely out of earshot, Yasmin leaned towards Carlos and whispered, "Quit stalling, you are driving me nuts."

"Well," he theatrically paused, "I think we should move the *Loco Lobo* away from Hidalgo Avenue to a waterfront location."

"What a great idea! But where?"

Chapter 4

April 3rd Cancun

Alfonso Fuentes flipped to a photo on his iPhone. He was obsessed with this woman. Jessica Sanderson was trim, with long blonde hair that spilled down her back, ending just above her firm ass. She had the bluest eyes he had ever seen.

Fuentes knew women were attracted to his fit body, deep-set brown eyes, short dark hair, and thick moustache. He had a pleasant face when he chose to smile, but he didn't think Jessica would agree. He had tried to kill her — twice.

Rafael Fernandez, his now-dead employer, had demanded that he eliminate the fourteen people in her group of friends and their children. In the mind of the drug lord this tight-knit set of islanders had interfered in his businesses on Isla Mujeres and needed to be taught an unforgettable lesson.

Fuentes had convinced his boss to let him kill only Jessica, whom he saw as the unofficial ringleader of the group. His argument was they didn't want the tourists to panic and shun the popular vacation area. The formerly trendy playground of Acapulco had suffered a terrible economic downturn caused by aggressive cartels. Fuentes didn't want the same thing to happen to their lucrative drug trade in the Cancun and Riviera Maya resorts.

Fernandez had snarled a response, "Do it. But if you screw up, you will be replaced." *Replaced* was his euphemism for a slow and painful death.

Fuentes first attempt to bump off Jessica had been at the wedding of her friends, Yasmin Medina and Carlos Mendoza. Her aunt had leaned forward at exactly the wrong moment, and he had shot her by mistake. She had survived, being rapidly transported to a critical care hospital in Cancun via the fast sport fishing boat that belonged to two of Jessica's friends.

The second attempt had been at the passenger ferry terminal as she exited a taxi. She and her family members had spent the night in Cancun waiting at the hospital while the staff fought to save her aunt's life. Jessica's ever-present scruffy beach-mutt had sensed a problem and raced straight at Fuentes, sinking his fangs deep into his calf muscles.

Fuentes fired a shot at his target and another at her dog, then ran for his motorcycle hampered by the mongrel still attached to his leg. He had booted the animal in the head, loosening its hold on his leg. As he gunned the big machine into the early morning traffic someone had tossed something hard and rough, bashing his unprotected skull. Momentarily stunned Fuentes felt the bike wobble beneath him, but he managed to wrestle it back on course and speed away. Fuentes stashed the motorcycle in his secret storage unit beside his white Sahara Jeep.

The following twelve hours had been harrowing. He was injured but didn't dare use the doctor who was on the *Don's* payroll. He knew he was marked for removal by his ruthless boss for failing to complete his assignment. He finally admitted to himself that on the second attempt he had deliberately missed; he was infatuated with the woman.

Watching the sunrise from a secluded beach he contemplated his next move. He had heard a car door slam, and then another. Resigned to dying on this tiny strip of sand he had slowly turned to face the two gunmen. He drew his pistol, aiming for the closest man, but before he could squeeze the trigger both of the assassins silently dropped to the ground in a mist of red.

Executed by snipers!

His pulse free-wheeled in his veins as he fled the scene, racing back to his storage unit. Fuentes slumped against his Jeep, his mind replaying the bizarre sequence of events. It was then that he remembered seeing a note on the passenger's seat.

He picked it up and read the computer-printed note.

This is your one chance. We helped you. Kill Fernandez and we will leave you alone — for now. Confirm with a photo to this number.

That was an easy decision; kill or be killed.

Rafael Fernandez had been overconfident in the abilities of his fledgling enforcers. He had not expected a very-much alive Fuentes to sneak into his secure compound and fire three bullets into his chest. The fourth bullet in his head was the insurance shot. A shocked grimace had twisted his dying face.

With a handful of loyal supporters Fuentes fought for and won the leadership of the drug cartel. He was now *Don* Alfonso, Señor Fuentes, *el Jefe*. But he still didn't have a clue as to who his mysterious benefactors were. His best guess was they were ex-Army snipers working for another cartel. *Why had they let him live?* Troubling questions chewed at his brain. *Who? Why? And when would they make their move against him?*

Chapter 5

April 3rd Isla Mujeres

"What do you mean my debit card has been cancelled? Why?" Jessica queried the bank employee. The conversation was frustrating, taxing her inadequate Spanish to the limit. Her body leaned towards the young woman sitting behind a black and chrome, inexpensive computer-workstation. Her name tag simply read Luci, no last name.

Luci nervously stammered in Spanish, "You had a suspicious charge on your card, so it was cancelled."

"What charge?"

"A gasoline purchase in Florida."

"When?" Jessica scrunched her eyebrows together, creating a pleat in the space between her eyes.

"Yesterday."

"Huh." Jessica leaned back, forcing herself to

relax a little. It wasn't Luci's fault; she was just doing her job. "Well, that definitely wasn't me. So, yes it was fraudulent."

"You made a withdrawal yesterday, and then the gas purchase showed up in Florida later on the same day. That's why the card was cancelled." Luci stumbled on with her explanation.

Jessica shook her head emphatically. "No, I tried to take out money. The message said: card not authorized."

"It shows that you took out two thousand pesos yesterday."

"No, I didn't," She shook her head, "And my friend Yasmin is my witness." Jessica could feel her frustration building again. She leaned forward to emphatically point a finger at one of the CCTV cameras recording the activity in the entrance lobby. "The bank has security cameras everywhere and the ATMs also record every transaction."

"Si, claro. We will investigate that charge as well."

"What do I do now?"

"We'll order you a new card, but it could take two or more weeks."

Jessica closed her eyes momentarily, and sighed. "I have to pay my rent, Luci, and I need *dinero*." Unlike when she lived in Canada and a debit card could be used for any purchase, including a cup of coffee and a chocolate donut at Tim Horton's, she seldom used her card in Mexico. It was normally only used for withdrawals, groceries, and the occasional purchase at Costco in Cancun. Still, it would be a pain in the butt to not have it available for a few weeks. It was just another annoying little problem to fix.

"I will help you to make a withdrawal," Luci said.

"Okay, thank you. Will I be reimbursed for the fraudulent withdrawal and the gas purchase?" She asked.

"That will take a few days to investigate, but yes I'm sure you will get the money back."

~

Several hours later Jessica arrived for her customary shift from four in the afternoon until their official closing time of midnight. Sometimes a few patrons lingered over their last drink order while she and Yasmin rolled down the security grille and tidied the restaurant for the morning staff, but usually she was home by one in the morning. The hours suited her lifestyle and the tips were normally better during the late afternoon shifts.

"Hola Jess," Yasmin waved briefly as she

headed into the storage area. The door partially closed behind her, muffling her voice while she continued speaking.

"What?" Jessica asked. "Sorry, I didn't hear you."

Yasmin reappeared, her arms loaded with two bottles of bloody Caesar mix, a jar of jalapeño-stuffed olives, and a long package of tiny white napkins. "I asked if you had sorted out your debit card problem."

"No, it's been cancelled. There was a withdrawal on my account yesterday morning and then someone purchased gas in Florida a few minutes later."

"Really? That's awful. Do you need money?"

"No thanks Yassy. Luci at the bank helped me make a withdrawal. She says it takes about two weeks for a new card." Jessica waggled her hand back and forth, "más o menos, more or less."

"Did she offer any explanation?"

Jessica snorted a laugh, "Ah, no. I am pretty sure the bank wants to keep it quiet that there are problems with the ATMs."

"Si, I am certain they do," Yasmin agreed, as she wrapped two long apron strings around her slim waist, and doubled them back around to her belly button, and tied a bow. "I can't remember, did I tell you about the little dust-up Carlos had this morning?" She asked.

"Dust-up?" Jessica playfully cocked her fists in a boxer's stance. "Was Carlos in a fight? I thought he'd outgrown that bad-boy stuff."

"It was more like a virtual brawl," Yasmin said, with wry chuckle.

Jessica dropped her hands, "What happened?"

"One of the administrators for an Isla Facebook group banned the use of Spanish for any posts."

"What!"

Yasmin nodded grimly, "His response exactly. The group's focus is Isla Mujeres Mexico and the administrator has banned the use of Spanish on the page!"

"It sounds discriminatory to me," Jessica said. "What did he do?"

"He blasted the ridiculousness of the policy in both English and Spanish, and then we removed ourselves, and the *Loco Lobo*, from the group."

"Good move," Jessica chuckled. "You would have been kicked off, anyway, for your insubordination."

"I am still infuriated about the policy. It's ludicrous," Yasmin sputtered. "This is our country and we speak Spanish."

"Well, you've heard me repeat many times a saying that an American friend taught me; this is not my country, I am a guest." Jessica said, giving Yasmin a light hug. "Sometimes visitors just don't get that simple concept."

Chapter 6

April 10th Cancun

"*Mierda!*" Detective Marco Cervera dropped another piece of paper onto his already cluttered desk. Constructed of inexpensive particleboard and abused by dozens of police detectives over the years the piece of furniture wobbled when he bumped a large knee against the edge. He instinctively reached out to steady the ever-present cup of coffee that threatened to tip its residue onto the stack of papers.

"*Que pasa* Marco?" Dante Toledo asked without raising his head. He was hunched over a stack of reports. Known as the twins, *Los Gemelos*, Cervera and Toledo habitually wore black suits, white shirts, skinny black ties and gleaming black shoes.

Partners in the Cancun State Police for several years, the men had become close friends. Cervera was pushing fifty. He was thick around the middle, and his short dark hair was flecked with grey. His fleshy face resembled a bewildered

Basset hound recently abandoned by his owners. Toledo on the other hand was a hard-faced Latino, a younger version of Tommy Lee Jones as Agent K in the 1990's spoof *Men in Black*.

"More problems with ATMs. Another report from that same bank on Isla Mujeres." Cervera lifted his coffee cup and inspected the cold, oily liquid. He set it down and shoved it aside. He felt his pockets, checking for money. Time to get a fresh cup from his favourite barista, Amelia.

"In case you forgot, hotshot, we're homicide detectives." Toledo glanced up with a wry smile twisting his face. "Why are you reading fraud reports?"

"My gut instinct is telling me this problem is escalating into something nasty." He stood up and straightened his tie. "I'm going for a coffee. You want another one?"

"Ah, your famous spare-tire is sending you clues again," Toledo teased his partner, as he dug in the drawer searching for his wallet. He pulled out a bill, and handed it across to Cervera. "Same as usual, black two sugars."

Cervera waved away the money, "My treat. You can buy next time." He ambled towards the stairway and headed to the main floor two flights below. It wasn't much in the way of exercise, but his darling Beatriz was worried about his love of food and cerveza. He had replied it was her fault because she was such an amazing cook. That comment had earned him a light smack on the shoulder, and a sexy kiss. The slap was because he had been cheeky, and the kiss said she loved him anyway.

Although most Mexicans worked long hours at physically hard jobs their diets mainly consisted of a tiny bit of protein, plenty of cheap, refined carbohydrates, and oodles of sweet, fizzy beverages. Diabetes had become a national epidemic since the introduction of carbonated soda pop in the 1920's.

Beatriz had shown him an internet article that she wanted him to read. The article stated the average Mexican drank one-hundred and sixty-three litres of pop a year, or a half-litre per day which contained thirteen teaspoons of sugar. Every single day. No wonder so many of his friends and family suffered from diabetes. He was trying to cut back, and he no longer added sugar to his innumerable cups of coffee necessary to get him through a work day. He also walked when he could. It was a start.

Outside the police station the sun felt good on his face. He walked the short distance, and pushed open the glass door. Amelia glanced up and smiled a greeting.

"Hola Marco," She said when it was his turn at the counter. "The same as usual?"

"Por favor, just black for me, and black with two sugars for Dante."

She grinned at him, "You're losing weight."

"Si, orders from mi esposa."

Amelia poured the coffees, pushed the lids on and placed the two packets of sugar on top of one of the containers. "Dante should cut down on his sugar too."

"He's skinny. He doesn't have to worry," Cervera said unconsciously rubbing a hand across his wide stomach.

"Sugar is bad for everyone," She said with the certainty of youth.

Cervera curbed his smirk, trying instead for an agreeable smile. In his experience the younger generation more often than not presumed they were smarter than their elders. He had made the same assumption when he was in his twenties. His nose was still a little off-centre from when his dad had adjusted his attitude with a powerful backhand smack.

He dropped his change into her tip container and picked up the coffees. "See you tomorrow, Amelia."

"Gracias. Hasta pronto."

Cervera pushed the glass door open with his hip while balancing the two very hot coffees, one in each hand. Thankfully Amelia had put one of those cardboard hand-protector thingies around each cup or he would have dropped them by now. *Damn they were hot!*

He strode as quickly as possible back to the station, and up the stairs. He didn't see his partner, so he set the coffee by his workstation. "Where's Toledo?"

"Baños." Another detective answered without looking up.

Cervera pulled off the coffee cover and tentatively took a sip. "Ow, shit." He put the cup down, hoping to remember to drink it before it too was forgotten and cold.

Toledo strolled back into the squad room. "Thanks for the coffee, Marco."

"Careful, it's boiling hot." Cervera pulled the two packets of sugar from his pocket and tossed them to Toledo. "Amelia says you should cut down on your sugar."

Toledo snatched the packets out of the air, and quirked a smile at his partner. "Since when is it her business what I eat or drink?"

"Sugar is bad for everyone," He answered, imitating Amelia's young voice.

Toledo laughed, tore the packets open and dumped them simultaneously into the hot brew. As he stirred his coffee with a dirty spoon, he asked. "This latest premonition your gut has, what's that about?"

"Let's take our drinks up to the roof. Beatriz is convinced I need to get more vitamin D. I can get some sun while our coffees cool." His level stare conveyed more than his words. *Not here.*

"Sounds like a plan."

The two men thumped their way up the staircase to the roof, and stepped out into the sunlight. Cervera pointed with his chin towards a corner where they could perch their butts on the concrete parapet and keep an eye on the doorway. He put one finger on his lips in a *keep quiet* gesture, set his coffee on the low wall then reached into a pocket for his phone. He powered it off, and indicated to Toledo to do the same.

Toledo complied then quirked his eyebrows up towards his hairline, "What's up?"

"You remember our *friend* Alfonso Fuentes?" He asked, putting sarcasm into the word friend. He was referring to the new kingpin of the Cancun cartel.

"Of course."

"After reading through the files I am certain the Romanian gang we have been hearing about lately is responsible for the big increase in ATM fraud. Fuentes won't stand for them working in his territory."

"No, he won't."

"Things could get messy, and we could have bodies piling up."

"Agreed."

"I'm not sure where our Captain's loyalties lie. Are you?"

"No, but why turn off the phones? Everyone knows where we are. They don't need to track us."

"Ah, my techie-nerd nephew recently clued me in on another way of checking on us. Every electronic device has a microphone-array that can be activated to listen in on conversations."

"Are you shitting me?" Toledo blurted out.

"No, I'm not," Cervera said with a decisive shake of his head. "Facebook, What's App, Google

Play ... all sorts of big companies can listen to your conversations, hear what TV programs you watch, or what music you play. With that kind of technology out there don't you think that maybe our employers can figure out a way to listen to us as well?"

"And you don't want anyone to connect us with Fuentes."

"Exactly."

Chapter 7

April 14th Cancun

Alfonso Fuentes' pupils expanded with rage until his eyes looked like bottomless black pits. Under the scrutiny of his intense glare his second-in-command Ventura Rodriquez nervously adjusted his weight from one foot to the other.

"What do you mean there are a dozen new ATMs in the hotel zone?"

"A new company has installed them all along the Kukulcan Boulevard, many within a hundred meters of the next one."

"How did you not know this was happening?"

"I'm sorry, Jefe. Our sources knew nothing about it until the ATMs were being installed."

"Someone is poaching in our territory. Find them!"

"Claro, *Don* Alfonso." Rodriquez turned and quietly exited the room, taking care not to disrespectfully slam the door.

Fuentes angrily leapt out of his chair and began pacing. It wasn't like Rodriquez to miss such a blatant encroachment of his domain. *Who had been paid off? What organization was behind this bold move? Had Rodriquez been bought off by another cartel?*

He flung open his office door and marched towards the kitchen where Esmeralda, the Guatemalan woman he had inherited along with the title of *Don*, was busy preparing the mid-day meal. As he neared, he saw her shoulders tighten, her focus pinned on the pot she was stirring. He slowed his pace and vainly tried to soften his expression.

"Buenos días, Esmeralda. Cómo estás?" He said pleasantly.

"Buenos días, *Don* Alfonso," She whispered, still staring at the stove.

"Señora, por favor," he said, "bring two cups of coffee and come to my office." He pointed back the way he had come.

"Si, of course, *Don* Alfonso," She bobbed her head without looking at him. She wasn't groveling, but she was panicky. He could see the joints in her fingers were white with tension as she gripped the large metal spoon.

"Bien." He turned and retreated back the way he had come, leaving the door open for her.

A few minutes later Esmeralda nervously entered his office and set down a heavy tray laden with a coffee urn, two cups, teaspoons, napkins, warm milk, a bowl of raw sugar and even a plate of her freshly baked goods. She must have scrambled to assemble it so quickly, he mused.

As she poured the coffee, he walked behind her and closed the door; she involuntarily flinched with a quick rabbit-like jerk. He curbed his snort of amusement. *I wouldn't invite you for coffee if I was going to slit your throat.*

"Gracias," He said politely and accepted the steaming cup of aromatic coffee. He had some idea of Esmeralda's history. Her father had sold her at a very young age to Rafael Fernandez, his now-dead predecessor. Esmeralda was quick to understand that she would eventually be replaced with a younger girl, and her future was bleak unless she could make herself indispensable.

Fernandez loved to eat good food but his housekeeper had been lazy and unimaginative with her food preparation. Whenever Fernandez wasn't using Esmeralda for his own pleasure, she trained herself to be a talented cook. She read books. She watched food programs on the television, and offered to do the shopping so that she could speak to other women in the market. Then the inevitable day arrived and the boss had pulled a new whimpering eleven-year-old child into his luxurious suite. Minutes later he tossed a few items of Esmeralda's clothing into the hallway and told her to find a place to sleep in the staff quarters. Fernandez then dismissed the older cook and told Esmeralda that housekeeping and food preparation were now her responsibilities.

She was just fifteen years old.

As the lieutenant to Fernandez, Fuentes had watched in amused admiration as Esmeralda quickly cleaned out a storage area, and hung a hammock. She added a small mirror, a wash basin and a place to hang her meager collection of clothing. In an unguarded moment Fuentes had noticed a look of pure relief, as she turned the key in the lock. This was her sanctuary, safe from the predatory males roaming the compound. He decided she had earned the right to a bit of privacy and warned the randy wolf-pups. *Leave her alone. Do not molest her.*

Fuentes pointed at the coffee urn, "Please pour yourself a cup of coffee and sit down."

The cook did as he instructed. She warily perched on the edge of the chair and concentrated her gaze on his desk.

"Esmeralda," He said, pretending not to notice as her hand trembled and spilled some of the coffee she was about to sip. "I have known you for several years, and yet I know nothing about you. What is your last name?"

"Benitez, *Don* Alfonso."

"Esmeralda Benitez, mucho gusto." He raised his coffee cup in a courteous salute. She was still a young woman, who despite her attempts to disguise her body with loose dresses and an assortment of sexless uniforms was, without question, gorgeous. Her dark eyes were luminous. Her mocha-coloured skin flawless. And unless she had recently cut her hair, he knew she was hiding a luxurious dark mane under her chef's cap. She was every Latino male's wet dream, except his. He lusted only for one woman.

"Gracias, Señor." Esmeralda cautiously let her eyes meet his for the briefest of moments then resumed her fascination with his desk.

"And where were you born?" He asked taking another sip of the delicious coffee.

"Antigua, Señor."

Fuentes curbed his irritation at her brief answers. She was terrified. He quietly sucked in a long breath willing himself to be patient with her.

"Antigua is a beautiful city, surrounded by many volcanoes."

"Si, *Don* Alfonso."

"Esmeralda, you work long hours preparing our delicious meals, cleaning the kitchen, plus keeping the house and the barracks tidy."

"It is my pleasure," She whispered.

"I have one more task for you." He put his cup back on its saucer and leaned forward. "Look at me please," He quietly commanded pinning her with his dark eyes.

Her eyes lifted to his face. He could see the resignation, the realization that her hard-won freedom was illusionary. She understood her fate was to work in a brothel. "Of course, Señor, anything you ask I will do," She whispered.

"I would like you to bring coffee to me every morning, and tell me what the men discuss when I am not in the room."

Her mouth dropped open. Her hand quickly stifled a cry of relief.

"I want you to be my eyes and ears. Do you understand?"

"Claro, *Don* Alfonso." She quickly dabbed her eyes, and straightened her spine.

"You will say nothing to the others," He demanded.

"No, never. I swore loyalty to you the day you became our *Don*."

"Yes, I remember," He said. At the time he had thought how she could be very useful. A female housekeeper was virtually invisible to the men and they felt free to express their complaints about their bosses. As a much younger enforcer he had experienced first-hand the grumbling and bitching that happened in the communal eating area. Once he was promoted to Fernandez's lieutenant, his arrival would cause a suspiciously rapid change in conversations to innocent subjects like women or sports teams.

"Bien. That is all for now."

"Gracias, *Don* Alfonso. Would you like me to leave the coffee and pastries for you?" She whispered.

He shook his head, "No gracias."

Esmeralda quietly scuttled out of the room, awkwardly balancing the large tray with one hand while she reached back to close the door behind herself.

Fuentes made no move to help her. He wanted her to remain respectful and not become overly confident of his protection. He wouldn't be the unbalanced sociopath that Fernandez had been; but he would kill anyone to maintain his nascent grip on the cartel.

Chapter 8

April 17th Isla Mujeres

"What do you think about this location for our new restaurant?" Carlos asked, as he pointed to a small marina complex located close to where Pedro and Diego berthed the *Bruja del Mar*. This was the third waterfront property that they had looked at in the last two weeks. It was located a little further north on Laguna Makax. It should have a great view of the sheltered waterway, but also of the bay and the mainland area.

Standing across the street from the fenced entrance, Yasmin studied the property. There wasn't much space for parking. The *Loco Lobo* was situated in Centro and the bulk of their customers stayed at nearby hotels and usually walked to the restaurant. This location was about two kilometers farther south, meaning more of their regulars would need a place to park.

On the plus side — the neighbourhood had an energetic vibe. There were several new places that had recently opened, or moved from the crowded downtown streets. The water view would be a bonus, but it came at a cost; more mosquitoes in the evenings and less wind so higher temperatures in the summertime.

"Can we look inside the gates?"

"Sure, they aren't locked. We'll just walk in, and if anyone questions us, we are looking for our sailing friends who are visiting the island." He reached for her hand. "There's a gap in the traffic, let's go."

Yasmin and Carlos hustled across the road, then she glanced back at the conga-line of golf carts streaming past. "I can't believe how much the traffic has increased in the last few years."

"Si, it's good and bad," He agreed. "Good for our business and bad for our peace and quiet. But the *carritos de golf* are better than all the big SUVs that are showing up on the island."

"Speaking of which, are you ever going to make up your mind about buying a new car with the insurance payout from your Porsche?" She asked, flicking an enquiring glance at him. "It's been almost eight months since your car was wrecked by the hurricane."

About to start down a short flight of stairs that led to the boat docks Carlos hesitated on the top step, and said. "It depends."

"On what?"

"You still haven't answered my question from a few weeks ago."

"What question?"

"Do you want a family?"

"When did you ask me that?" She stammered.

His mischievous grin lifted his cheeks and crinkled his eyes, "The night we stayed at the Rolandi Hotel to celebrate our marriage." He cocked one eyebrow, "We drank a lot of champagne that night."

"I vaguely remember sharing two bottles of champagne and then I had a killer hangover the next morning."

"You were so noisy in the bathroom I thought you had morning sickness," He grinned.

"I was over-served!"

"You were puking up your toenails," He laughed.

She turned a sheepish grin on him, "Was I really that bad? I don't remember."

"Don't worry, I've done worse." He put his arm around her and pulled her close for a kiss, "But there was definitely no romance that night. You were passed out and ... you didn't smell so good."

Yasmin elbowed his ribs, "Jerk."

"Still avoiding my question?"

She smiled and hurried down the stairway to the docks. "Buy me dinner at Limón tonight and I'll tell you."

Carlos pulled out his phone and quickly thumbed a message to Limón's Facebook page, booking a table for two at seven-thirty. Charrissa Gillingham confirmed almost immediately. "Done. No more excuses," He muttered.

Yasmin continued walking along the wharf, half-listening to him mumble to himself while she visualized the changes necessary to turn this property into a happening place.

The small building would have to be torn down and a purpose-built structure put in its place. They would need a big shaded deck with comfortable seating to take advantage of the view. The sunny locations could be more casual with colourful umbrellas, bright plastic chairs and flowering plants. A big bar with space for at least two bartenders to work without tripping over each other was a necessity.

They would need a musicians' area for sure, sheltered from the intense sun or the occasional tropical downpour with lots of electrical outlets for instruments, equipment and lighting.

In the last ten years the annual Island Time Music Festival had created a thriving atmosphere for local performers as well as drawing dozens of Nashville singers, songwriters, and bands. Profits from the popular festival were donated to The Little Yellow School House, a local school for disadvantaged children, kids who suffered from emotional, mental or physical disabilities.

The event had rapidly grown from four small venues in Centro to several larger locations scattered along the length of the island. In the lead-up to the five days of the festival and the after-party gigs the island pulsed with music and energy for two weeks. With the new location they could tap into the vibrant music scene.

"What do you think?" Carlos asked.

"I love the location, but we would be starting from scratch. Are you sure you want to do this?"

"Yes, but only if you agree. This will be a huge sacrifice for both of us in time, energy and money."

Yasmin smiled at him. "We have to sit down with a calculator and really think this through." *And this will change my answer about having a family.*

~

"Oh my God, that was wonderful," Yasmin said as she laid her knife and fork on the side of the plate.

"It is my pleasure," Sergio Martinez said, as he hovered beside her elbow.

"Muy rico!" Carlos said kissing the tips of his fingers. He leaned back to allow a waiter to remove their dishes.

"I am glad you enjoyed it." Sergio lifted the bottle of Argentinian Malbec and topped up Yasmin's wine, and then emptied the remainder into Carlos' glass.

"Now, may we bring you *un postre*, a dessert?"

"No, no. Please I couldn't eat another bite." Yasmin held her hands up.

"Do you have your Chocolate Masterpiece available tonight?" Carlos asked.

"You are in luck. We do have it this evening."

"One please … and two forks." He winked at Sergio. Yasmin would weaken and want to share. The dark chocolate sphere stuffed with chocolate mousse was guaranteed to shock a person's pancreas, but it could be argued that the handful of fresh berries decorating the plate were healthy antioxidants.

Yasmin let out a theatrical moan, "That's not fair! You know I love that dessert."

Sergio's white teeth flashed as he laughed at her comical protest. He relayed the order to a server and turned his attention to the meat sizzling on a large gas grill.

Yasmin leaned back and sipped her wine. "I absolutely love the cozy, romantic atmosphere here in the courtyard with the stars above us."

"Me too. That property we looked at today could be split into two sections. We could have a very classy upper deck, and a rocking party space on the lower deck."

"Or vice versa. Keep the lovers closer to the water and the crazy people nearer the bar."

"Good idea. Now, enough stalling." He said taking her hand. "What's your answer?"

"Yes ..."

"But ...?"

"We can't afford children and a new restaurant."

They stopped talking as Jose placed the dessert in the middle of the table and carefully laid a clean fork and spoon in front of each of them. "Gracias," They murmured.

Carlos gently stroked his thumb across the palm of her hand and held her gaze. "Carina, we'll figure it out. It wouldn't be easy, but we can do both." Then he laughed and added, "Unless of course you are planning to have twelve, thirteen, or maybe fourteen babies ... then it might be a bit of a problem."

"Sometimes you are such an ass," She said shaking her head, and grinning. "Two would be perfect. Not two dozen."

"Two it is."

"And a vehicle that will hold four people," Yasmin added.

Carlos laughed, "Si, we'll buy a sensible family vehicle of your choice, carina." He raised his glass and smiled at her. "To us and a happy future."

"To us! I love you more every day," Yasmin replied, lightly clinking her glass against his, then sipping a small amount of wine. "Now, out of my way! I need some of that chocolate!"

Chapter 9

April 22nd Isla Mujeres

"Hola." An unfamiliar voice called from outside Jessica's front door.

She turned off the kitchen tap and set a tiny dish of fresh water on the countertop for her resident gecko, Geek, who lived behind her refrigerator. If she didn't leave him his own supply of water, he would try to drink from Sparky's larger water bowl. After two near-drowning mishaps he now had his personal gecko-sized dish.

Geek was her ecologically friendly bug-catcher, coming out after dark to gulp down mosquitoes and lick up ants. Occasionally during the night, she would hear his *chuk-chuk-chuk* calling for a mate or warning other geckos away from his territory.

Drying her hands on a bit of paper towel Jessica pondered the mystery of Geek. Was he a male or a female? How do you tell the sex of an almost translucent tiny lizard clinging to the ceiling? Yesterday she had spotted two recently hatched geckos clinging to her walls – very likely the off-spring of Geek and ...

"Hola?" The man repeated with a tinge of impatience.

"Oh crap, I forgot," She said as she hurried towards her front doorway.

"Hola, buenos días." Pulling open her front door Jessica stared thoughtfully at the stranger. *Who's he?* He was sitting on a moto that had two saddle bags stuffed with what appeared to be stacks of white envelopes. He wasn't the regular mailman who rode a white moto with pink and green *Correo de Mexico* decals displayed on both sides of the gas tank.

"Señorita Yessica Sanderson?" The man asked stumbling over her name.

"Si. Yo soy Jessica."

"¿Tienes identificación? ¿Un pasaporte?"

"My passport? Why?"

He held up a business-sized envelope with the return address of the head office of the bank she used. "A new card for you," He said in Spanish. "I need to see your passport."

"Okay, one minute." She turned away from the door, "Come inside Sparky," She said. If she didn't keep him in the house, he would investigate the moto and affix his individual brand of cologne to the exterior of the saddle bags. He reluctantly followed her into the house.

She opened her small safe and removed her Canadian passport. It irritated her that Mexicanos never had to produce this type of document for identification. Their voting card from the Instituto Nacional Electoral was sufficient. She sighed and reminded herself, yet again; *this is not my country. I am a guest.*

She passed the booklet to the deliveryman and watched as he carefully copied down the long and complicated number. He handed her a pen and the official receipt and asked her to print her name, then sign and add the date. He carefully scrutinized the two signatures, then seemingly satisfied that she was who she purported to be returned her passport. That done she politely offered him a small bottle of cold water and closed the door.

Jessica tore open the envelope and removed the new debit card that was glued to the enclosed letter. She fanned face with the card and said to Sparky, "Now, all I have to do is waste and hour or so in the bank while they activate this."

"First, I have to wait in line for one of the employees who were allowed to assist with changing a PIN. Next, I get to sit at their desk and endure a set of security procedures and then finally — activate my card. The only way to shorten the time is to be waiting in front of the glass entrance doors at fifteen minutes before opening time. That way I can be the first client through the doors and I can ask Luci to help me with this."

Sparky's expression said he knew exactly what she was talking about, but he was probably just hoping for another ride before she went to work.

"It's a good thing most people don't think it's crazy to talk to a pet."

Sparky grinned. His long tongue lolled out of his wide mouth.

~

Diego Avalos shut down the twin engines of the sport fishing boat the *Bruja del Mar*. Pedro and he had offloaded their customers plus their piles of expensive cameras and custom-fitted wetsuits at the yacht club docks behind the Bally Hoo Restaurante, and then taken the *Bruja* to her home berth for the night. She needed a thorough cleaning and re-provisioning in preparation for the next charter.

"Hey, did I tell you I saw that dick-head Ryan Whitecross back on the island?" Diego asked. He opened a storage locker and pulled out a hose, tossing an end to his brother-in-law Pedro Velazquez. Pedro attached it to a spigot on the dock.

"You ready for water?" Pedro asked.

"Si," Diego gave him a thumbs up.

"When did you see Whitecross?" Pedro asked. He turned on the tap and stepped aboard the boat.

Pedro's short-legged, physique contrasted with Diego's long-legged body. Neither man had ever set a foot inside a gym; they were wide shouldered and muscular from hard physical work. Pedro had a classic Maya blade shaped nose, sculpted lips and deep-set eyes. His head was bald by choice, not genetics. Diego had thick dark hair, cut short. His hair was straight when short but frizzy curls erupted if he neglected his monthly hair cut.

"Yesterday. I guess it slipped my mind." Diego did a visual check to ensure all the salon windows were closed then opened the nozzle and sprayed fresh water on the superstructure. His crooked nose and dark eyes lent him a menacing air until he smiled, then his wide grin and mischievous sparkle in his eyes hinted at a wicked sense of humour and an adventurous soul.

"Jessica is going to be pissed off." Pedro moved away from the cascading water, waiting until Diego was finished. "Or, as she says royally-pissed-off!" Pedro said with a hint of laughter in his voice.

"No shit. I thought we made it quite clear to him that he wasn't welcome on the island." Diego shut off the hose, and looped it over the railing. He reached in the bucket for a wet soapy cloth, and noticed the printing. It was a tattered t-shirt, a giveaway memento from the first anniversary of *Facebar*. Situated across the street from *La Tablita,* and on the second floor of a windowless building, *Facebar* was very much a locals' hangout. The staff kept track of drinks by leaving the bottles and glasses on the table until the clients were done. Some of their regulars had cases stacked beside their tables for their empty beer bottles. *Always lots of laughs there. Fun times*.

"Are you sure it was him?" Pedro asked, dragging Diego's attention back to the conversation about Whitecross. "It's been a couple of years since we *suggested* that he leave and not come back."

"Si, I'm sure." They had their routine and neither man had to think about what to do next. They worked smoothly together, and gossiped to pass the time. "When he saw me, he turned and actually ran into a restaurant." Diego answered, smiling at the memory of Whitecross' expression. "I think if I had followed him, he would have messed his pants."

"Maybe he was on one of the day-tripper boats from the hotel zone in Cancun. Sightseeing with other friends."

"Yeah, maybe."

"At least he isn't dangerous. Stupid yes, but a murderer like his buddy Kirk Patterson or Kyle Johnson or whatever the hell his real name was, I don't think so," Pedro said.

"Still, you have to wonder what would possess him to return. Whitecross admitted that he belatedly discovered Patterson's plan to rape and murder Yasmin, plus Patterson intended to steal any of the pirate's stash that Sparky and the ladies dug up." Diego tossed the cloth back in the bucket, splashing sudsy water onto the deck, "If I get my hands on him, I just might feed his ass to the sharks."

"After Jessica kicks him in the *cojones*," Pedro amended with a loud laugh.

"With Yasmin's help."

Chapter 10

April 23 Cancun

"Si, bueno," Dacey Uicab snatched up his cell phone when he heard the distinctive ringtone.

"This is your tia, your auntie," A deep masculine voice said. "Expect a delivery in fifteen minutes."

"Buenos días, Tia Rosa. Cómo está?" He said to dead air. His caller had already disconnected, but Dacey continued to chatter into the phone while he eyed his wife. She had her lazy butt glued to the sofa, again, watching her *telenovelas.* She watched so much television she could barely find the time in her busy schedule to scrape together a basic meal for him.

"Si, of course Tia Rosa. I would love to visit, but I am so busy at work," He continued his one-sided conversation.

"Lo Siento, someone is at our door," He said hearing the unique knock and the sound of hurried footsteps moving away from the door. Another delivery. "Claro, adios, Tia.

Everything was working perfectly — for him. Every week an envelope, fat with money in a variety of denominations, would be pressed into his hand as he passed Emanoil in the street, or slyly enclosed in a newspaper by Ionut and dropped on his table in a café. The new skimmers were delivered to his apartment door. His wife never once asked why his auntie called him so frequently or who was at the door. As for accidentally finding the devices stuffed in the bottom of his tool carrier, that would take a miracle. She wasn't the least bit interested in what he did for work but she had noticed that he wasn't sleeping well, and twice had asked why he was sitting bolt upright in bed with the light on. He'd claimed it was indigestion caused by spicy tacos.

His biggest worry was getting caught. His second biggest problem was keeping the extra dough hidden from her. He didn't want her asking awkward questions, or spending more in an attempt to impress her friends. He had been cautiously using it for small purchases, or sometimes buying better quality lunches for himself, or keeping the gas tank full on their crappy old car. *Maybe he should buy a newer car? No, much too obvious.*

A hectoring voice inside his head said, *Maybe, you should stop being such a wimp and find yourself a woman who truly appreciates you.*

~

Later in the afternoon, Dacey Uicab strode into the bank, pretending he didn't have a care in the world and that life was good, very good. As long as he could keep his fear under control, inserting the Bluetooth skimmers into the ATM readers was easy-peasy. A dream job.

After his terrifying abduction and the encounter with *The Voice*, Dacey had not been taken back to the Romanians' headquarters in the deserted office building. Instead everything was handled remotely by either Emanoil or Ionut. He couldn't have found the nameless building even if someone had paid him a million dollars. His exit was much like his entrance; hooded and transported in the white van. The only difference was his hands were not secured by plastic straps, and his tool bag contained six of the remarkable skimmers.

The man they referred to as *Bos* remained anonymous. Fine by him, Dacey was happy to never speak to the man again, much less meet him face to face. If Emanoil was being truthful anyone who saw the boss, other than his trusted associates, was due to be killed for one indiscretion or another. Talking too much. Flashing cash. Whatever the supposed violation, it was a death sentence when you met the man in charge.

The company that he worked for had the contract to maintain machines at a number of banks on a regular basis. He had managed to convince most of the bank managers that with all the ATM scams he should check more frequently. "And please," he had helpfully suggested to each manager, "if there were problems just call me on my private number for a quicker response time."

Most of the victims of the scam were vacationers, busy with exploring the Mayan Riviera or eating and drinking their way through the all-inclusive buffets. They typically wouldn't notice the extra charges on their debit cards until they returned home. Locals and part-time residents tended to be more vigilant and quickly complained about fraudulent charges to the bank staff.

When he received a frantic phone call from a branch manager, Dacey would scurry to fit in an extra service call. He would quickly remove the skimmers, declare everything was fine and return a week later to re-install the readers. Tomorrow would be his third trip to Isla Mujeres. He planned to insert the devices that he had removed the week before.

Eventually he would have to find a safe place to stash the money but for the interim it was pushed deep into his new tool satchel. It had a stout strap that crossed his chest and held the bag close to his body. Some of his workmates had razzed him, calling it a man-bag as if he was using a purse. He could take the ribbing, he just hoped no one figured out how much money he was carrying. Or why he had so much cash.

Yesterday when he had stopped by the office to pick up a few supplies he had seen a co-worker staring at him with a quizzical look on his face.

"Dacey, got a minute?" The man had hollered, gesturing with a beckoning motion.

Dacey pretended to answer his phone and with a friendly wave at his colleague had rushed off to attend to a fictitious emergency call.

~

"I have some info for you about the new ATMs in the hotel zone," A voice murmured over the phone.

"Momentito," Ventura Rodriquez replied. He recognized the voice as belonging to Lionel Hau, one of the ATM service technicians who was on their payroll. He covered the microphone and lightly rapped his knuckles on the door to the *jefe's* office.

"Adelante! Come in," Fuentes replied.

Rodriquez pushed open the door and held up his thumb and forefinger in the wait a moment signal. "I recognize your voice, Lionel," He said, then activated the speaker function on his phone and set it on the desk so that Fuentes could listen to the conversation.

Fuentes silently motioned for his lieutenant to sit in the chair across from him.

"What information do you have?" Rodriguez asked. His voice was firm and demanding.

"The ATMs are being installed by Romanians," Hau replied.

"Romanian?" Rodriquez replied with an unguarded note of surprise in his voice. His eyes sought Fuentes. This information was new to both of them.

"Si, they have also approached a few service technicians about installing skimmers in the machines."

"How do you know, Lionel?" Rodriquez queried.

There was an empty silence. He leaned closer to the phone and repeated the question with a little more heat in his voice, "How. Do. You. Know. Lionel?"

"They abducted me and demanded I work for them," Hau whispered. His fear was audible, present in every word that he murmured.

"And what did you say?"

"I was scared to death. *Lo siento mucho*, I said yes."

"You agreed to work for them?" Rodriquez could feel waves of anger radiating from Fuentes. He kept his eyes focussed on the phone, avoiding his boss's judgemental glare.

"They said if I didn't, I wouldn't leave the building alive," The technician stammered, "I have more information about the operation, but I want out. I need to move my family away from here. Far away." Hau implored, "Please Señor Rodriquez, please help me."

Rodriquez sucked in a breath and quietly exhaled. "I will call you back in twenty minutes, from a different number." He ended the call and shifted his gaze to Fuentes. "As you heard Lionel Hau is working with the Romanians but he wants to get away from them."

"Is he worth the effort?"

"Perhaps," Rodriguez temporized. He didn't want to defend Hau's actions. The little weasel could easily give the Romanians confidential information about their organization. That would infuriate Fuentes and possibly lead to his own death. No, he'd wait to hear what Hau had to say, then decide what to do with him.

"We should at least find out what he knows," Rodriguez added, noncommittally.

Chapter 11

April 23 Cancun

Fuentes leaned back in his chair and propped an ankle on his other knee while observing Rodriquez question Lionel Hau about the Romanians. He was watching via a closed-circuit camera with an audio feed.

The thin young man had rings of sweat under his arm pits. He frequently swiped at his face with the sleeve of his shirt. His left knee jiggled up and down, and his eyes bounced around as he babbled about being abducted, hooded and threatened.

"Tell me why you think Dacey Uicab is working for the Romanians?"

"He's become secretive and answering a lot of emergency service calls on his private cellphone."

"What else?"

"He has recently started to wear a satchel close to his body, as if he is protecting something valuable."

Rodriquez pointed at a similarly styled bag laying at Hau's feet."

"Like that one?"

Despite his coffee-toned skin the technician turned pale, as his eyes flickered to the bag. "Yes, like mine," He mumbled, as he wiped sweat from his face.

Rodriquez reached over and picked it up, reaching deep inside to pull out a thick wad of bank notes. "Interesting." His fingers riffled through the money.

"I was going to give it to *Don* Alfonso," Hau quickly said, as proof of what I am telling you."

"Si, of course you were."

"I was. It's my proof that they are paying technicians to install ATM skimmers."

"What's the name of the boss?" Rodriquez asked. He set the bag on the table beside his elbow, too far for Hau to reach. The message was clear; you won't be getting this back.

"He said I didn't need to know. I am telling you the truth," Hau squeaked. "Por favor, you have to believe me."

"Describe the men who abducted you?"

"Tall, thin, short dark hair, beards. I've already told you this, twice."

A cold smile twitched on Rodriquez's face, "Si, but like the policía we believe that describing your assailants again will help you remember more details. Continue."

"They looked like they could be relatives."

"Last names?"

"They told me I didn't need to know, but ...," he looked as if he was trying to drag up an elusive bit of information from the recesses of his memory, "Bilea. Yes, I overheard someone in the warehouse refer to Emanoil as Bilea, as if it was his nickname, or maybe his surname."

"See, you did remember more information," Rodriquez said. "Now, let's go through it again."

"*Por favor*," whimpered Hau. "I have to get back to work before my boss wonders where I am."

"Soon," Rodriquez reassured Hau.

Fuentes listened to Rodriquez temporize. The technician would remain where he was until Fuentes was satisfied there was no more information to be gained. Then Hau would be disposed of, or secretly transported to another city with his family. It all depended on whether or not he could be trusted to stay quiet about Fuentes' interest in the Romanians. He reached out a tapped a key on the CCTV control board, sending a short bleep through the speaker in the interview room. It was a signal to Rodriquez that he wanted to speak to him.

Rodriquez lifted his eyes to the camera to indicate he had heard.

"I'll be right back."

"Please," Hau's eyes were filled with tears. "I've done nothing wrong. I was terrified of the Romanians." He seemed to know his fate was about to be decided.

Rodriquez just lifted a hand in a stop signal, picked up the satchel then closed and locked the door behind himself.

"Well?" Fuentes asked. With the microphone turned off he could see, but not hear, Hau's tortured sobs.

"I think we should move him. He came to us. We didn't have to hunt him down." Rodriquez handed the bag containing the money to his boss. "There is about fifty thousand pesos inside."

Fuentes set it aside. Fifty thousand pesos was small change in his world, "Round up his family and send them out tonight." He rested his hand on the leather sack, "This will cover their relocation expenses."

"Where to?"

"Send him to Cervantes' organization, the Cartel Jalisco Nueva Generación."

"He won't last a week with that group." Rodriguez appeared to regret his retort, and hurried to explain. "Lo siento Jefe. I am not disagreeing with you. I meant it might be a waste of money to move him to that group."

Clearly disinterested in Hau's fate, Fuentes replied, "Maybe he will survive, or maybe he won't. It's better than the alternative of a guaranteed death if he stays here."

~

Fuentes called, "Adelante." The light knock on his door signaled that his housekeeper was asking permission to enter his office.

He remained seated, his inter-laced hands resting lightly on his favourite possession, an exquisite desk crafted from the Zapote trees in the Yucatan. The dense pieces of lumber were shot through with dramatic streaks of dark-chocolate brown and golden-yellow tones. A feeling of power and strength emanated from wood. It had belonged to his predecessor.

As was her habit Esmeralda balanced the tray with one hand while she opened the door, carefully set her burden on his desk and then turned to quietly close the door.

"Buenos días, *Don* Alfonso," She whispered, then poured him a cup of strong coffee, adding just a touch of hot milk and placed it by his right hand.

She poured a cup for herself and glanced at him, seeking permission to sit down.

"Por favor," He nodded, and waved a hand at the chair on the other side of the desk.

After a couple of attempts at mundane sociable conversation Fuentes had given up. She was plainly terrified of his reputation and he was quite confident she would not deceive him.

"What have you to report today?" He asked. Her cup rattled on her saucer. Interesting; she must have overheard something that could make him angry. He waited.

"I ... I am sorry, *Don* Alfonso," She stuttered, then searched for a safe place to set her cup.

As she dithered Fuentes noted that a small end table would solve her ridiculous dilemma. She appeared to be worried about her own safety, not wanting to be within striking distance of his hard fists. She finally decided to set it on the floor beside her chair instead of standing up and placing it back on the tray.

"Esmeralda, tell me," He said. He studied her beautiful face; so young, but etched with worry and fear.

"Some of the men are talking about working for the Romanians." Her hands were tightly clenched together in her lap, preventing them from displaying her obvious distress.

"Why?"

"More money, Señor." She kept her head bent, aiming her speech into her lap. "A lot more money."

"How do they know?"

"The one they call *Conejo*, Rabbit has been approached by the gang."

Fuentes held her gaze, searching for any sign that she might be lying to just get rid of *Conejo*. He was an annoying little *pendejo* that continually pushed the boundary of sexual assault despite Alfonso's previous warning to leave Esmeralda alone. She was definitely apprehensive, but she didn't appear to be deliberately lying.

"Thank you. I will deal with him later today. I don't want him to associate our visits with his predicament," Fuentes said, watching her blanch at the implied threat.

"I didn't mean for him to be harmed, *Don* Alfonso." Uncharacteristically, her eyes met his.

"It's not your concern," He answered, quietly. "The men need to be reminded of the rules."

Chapter 12

April 24th Isla Mujeres

"Good morning beautiful," Diego said, giving Jessica a buss on her cheek.

"Mornin' sweet cheeks," She responded. It was their standard greeting that Diego's wife Cristina knew was a harmless joke between the two friends. "What's up? You don't usually drop by my casa this early in the day.

"Nothing, just mooching a cup of coffee," He said as he squeezed his broad body past her, moving into her combination kitchen-living area.

Jessica rolled her eyes, "Right. Nothing. I'll make a fresh pot of coffee and then you *will* tell me what's going on."

"Hey Sparky, how's it hanging?" Diego said as he sat on the sofa, and patted his leg to beckon him closer. "Have you been a good boy lately?"

"Don't change the subject," She spoke over her shoulder as she filled the glass carafe with purified water and dumped it into the back of the coffeemaker. Next she added a paper filter, and two generous scoops of dark roasted grounds, and tapped the switch. "Okay, why are you at my house so early in the morning?"

"It's probably nothing," He continued to concentrate on scratching and patting Sparky.

"Diego! Quit stalling." She crossed her arms and leaned back against her kitchen countertop.

He met her blue-eyed stare and sighed, "I saw Ryan Whitecross on the island a couple of days ago."

"What the hell is he doing back on Isla?"

"Maybe he was on one of the day-tripper boats from Cancun," Diego repeated Pedro's remark.

"If he is back on the island, I will hunt him down and beat the crap out of him." Whitecross had been in her house, and in her bed. At the time she didn't know that Whitecross was pals with an escaped killer who was wanted in the USA for murdering several women, a long-haul driver and two sheriff's deputies. The thought still made her nauseous.

"Si, I get why you are angry Jess, but remember he didn't know anything about Kyle Johnson aka Kirk Patterson's background."

"So, *he* says!" She growled.

"Just be on your guard until we figure out what's going on."

Jessica huffed a curse, then jerked the carafe out of the machine before it had finished brewing and splashed fresh coffee into turquoise mugs. She jammed the glass carafe back under the spigot as it continued to sputter hot water over the grounds. She sloshed a bit of milk to both mugs plus a bit of sugar for Diego.

"You are going to break your favourite mug," Diego teased. The metal spoon clanked noisily against the ceramic as Jessica vigorously stirred the contents. She was beating the hell out of the coffee cup for such a meagre amount of sugar.

She tossed the spoon in the sink with a loud metallic clatter, "I just can't believe he would have the nerve to show his face on the island again." She handed him his coffee and plunked into her comfy armchair. She noticed Sparky cast a speculative look in her direction. He seemed to be deciding if he should risk snuggling her, or stay close to Diego's reassuring hand. She stuck her tongue out at her pup, "Traitor."

Diego's wide grin creased his face. "He thinks you are angry at him."

"I know," Her tantrum had fizzled out. Jessica patted her leg, "Come here sweetie." Sparky tucked his tail and sidled over to Jessica. "I'm not mad at you. I'm upset at a stupid guy." She smiled into his human-like eyes. "I love you, my little Sparkinator."

"And, of course, he knows exactly what you are saying."

"Yes, he does. He's a very smart boy." She slurped her coffee, and looked at Diego over the rim of her cup. "What do you honestly think Whitecross is up to?"

"No idea, but if I see him again, I'll have a little *chat* with him and find out."

~

Diego slid into his Jeep, pulling his thick thighs under the steering wheel, wishing yet again that he had purchased the tilt-up option. He didn't want Jessica to worry about Whitecross being on the island, but all the same she needed to know the guy was around. Hopefully the guy wouldn't decide to emulate his dead, but not lamented friend, Kirk Patterson.

He swung the vehicle onto the perimeter road, headed towards the marina where they berthed their sport-fishing boat. The *Bruja del Mar* needed a good cleaning and her regular maintenance.

Next week they had a photography charter booked for a group of repeat clients; a boisterous, group of guys from Calgary Alberta who wanted to swim with the whale sharks. They were disappointed to learn that whale shark season didn't start until late May, but Diego had promised to show them the sea turtles at Punta Sur. The giant turtles were starting to arrive for the annual mating free-for-all where the two currents met at the end of the island. He had tried to delay the group's arrival until later in June when there would be more turtles, plus whale sharks, but their busy work schedules didn't coincide with those dates. So, May 1st it was.

"*Maldito!*"

An erratically operated golf cart sped past him. Plastered on the side of the unit was a large logo with the rental company's name and the cart's number. The vehicle rocked from side to side as the driver swerved out and around his Jeep. His three shirtless passengers hooted and waved beer cans aloft in a brazen greeting.

"Hola amigo!"

"What the hell are they playing at?" Diego muttered, not acknowledging their greeting. They were either still drunk from the night before, or had started partying at sunup.

Driving one-handed the driver tipped back his can of beer and poured the remainder down his throat. He lobbed his empty can over the roof and onto the sidewalk. It bounced twice and settled in the tangled undergrowth, joining a collection of smashed beer bottles and crumpled beverage containers.

Just ahead of the small cart was a long black pickup truck with three dark-clad individuals inside the cab. *Policía. At least the idiots will slow down now.* Dumbfounded, Diego watched as the driver of the cart sped up attempting to hit the bumper of the police vehicle. He missed.

Diego eased off the gas, waiting for a reaction from the cops.

The truck and its occupants continued traveling sedately north as if nothing had happened.

Urged on by his companions the driver tried again to ram the backend of the pickup.

Still no reaction.

After a failed third attempt the driver of the police vehicle signalled and turned onto a side road, avoiding the situation entirely.

Diego's mouth dropped open, "Un-freaking-believable!"

The occupants of the golf cart whooped a victory yell and continued on their reckless journey.

Diego sighed, and signalled left. He had to get away from the idiots before he lost his temper. With his luck he would be charged with assault after pummeling a bit of sense into the *estúpidos pendejos*.

He wasn't sure who he wanted to pummel first; the drunken idiots, or the policía who deliberately ignored the situation.

Either way, his buddy Sergeant Felipe Ramirez of the policía municipal was going to get an earful.

Chapter 13

April 24th Cancun

Conejo, Rabbit, was a perfect nickname for the homely, bucktoothed twenty-two-year-old who was tied to a chair in the warehouse. He was an incongruous sight with blood, snot and tears leaking over his heavily tattooed face and chest. He had given up pretending he was tough. He looked like a terrified teenager.

"Iktan, you know how this ends." Fuentes said using the young man's real name, the Mayan word for Clever. His poor deluded mother apparently had a grandiose dream for her new baby boy. "Either you will die slowly, or you will die quickly, but you *will* die for betraying my trust."

"I didn't betray you, *Don* Alfonso. I swear on the life of my sainted mother, I did not betray you." Unable to drag air through his smashed nose, he breathed heavily through his mouth. "Please, I'm begging you, believe me."

"That is a lie, Iktan," Fuentes said, his voice flat and cold as he precisely enunciated each word. "You encouraged the others to help the Romanian thugs take over my territory. I want information, a location, names, and descriptions."

Conejo hung his head, "I ...I don't remember their names," he stuttered.

"I'm in no hurry. We will take as long as necessary for you to remember." Fuentes said leaning back in his chair. He deliberately reached for a bottle of cold water, uncapped it and took a long and satisfying drink. "You are not leaving this building alive. The sooner you give me the information the sooner your pain will end." He placed the bottle where Iktan could watch the condensation sliding down the plastic and pooling on the table. The man involuntarily licked his lips.

Fuentes picked up the Taser that rested beside his elbow. "Now, shall we start again?" Fuentes pointed the device at Iktan's crotch but before he could press the switch the man shrieked out a name.

"Emanoil Bilea!"

"Very good, who else?" Fuentes asked, delicately caressing the button with his thumb. His dark eyes remorselessly searched Iktan's face. He appeared to have resigned himself to betraying the Romanians.

"Ionut Pirjol."

Fuentes resisted the urge to glance at Rodriquez. This was good, a last name for the other man. "And who is the boss?"

Iktan's eyes filled with tears. "If I tell you I am a dead man." He blubbered.

"Iktan, Iktan. How many times do I have to tell you? You are already a dead man." Fuentes' tone implied he was repeating a tiresome lesson to a very young child. "Who is the boss?"

"Bortos. Adrian Bortos," Iktan whimpered.

"Description," Fuentes demanded.

"I don't know how to describe him, he's average. Brown hair, brown eyes, pale skin. About my height. A little pudgy around the middle. Just an average middle-aged guy."

"Tattoos? Birthmarks? Scars?"

"No," Iktan replied. "Wait … he has a mole on his left cheek."

"Where?"

"Near the side of his nose, I think." Forgetting he was tightly secured to the chair, Iktan reflexively twitched his damaged left hand in a futile attempt to point to the approximate location of the mole.

"What else?"

"Nothing. He just looks a regular guy who works in an office cubicle of a big company. An out of shape nobody."

"Where is their base of operations located?"

"It's an empty office building on the road towards the airport turnoff. It's old with a faded sign. Only the last four letters are visible: otes." Iktan spewed out the words. His brain seemed to be working faster than his tongue could form the sounds.

Fuentes sat staring at the man. *Was this the truth? Or was it a last defiant one-finger salute to his tormentors?* "Who do you love the most in all the world, Iktan? Your sainted mother?" Fuentes taunted Iktan with the same expression he had used, vowing that he hadn't betrayed his boss. "Or, do you love your four-year-old daughter Emma more?"

The terror in the man's eyes was eerily similar to that of a rabbit spellbound by the headlights of an on-rushing vehicle. "My daughter," He whispered.

"If you are lying to me, she will die, here, in front of you."

"No, please. I am telling the truth. Please leave Emma alone."

Fuentes turned to Rodriguez, "Get the kid."

"No!" Iktan screamed.

"And gag this *pendejo* before you leave. I'm tired of listening to him." Fuentes stood up and skimmed a disinterested glance at his captive. He would return to his questioning once they had the girl. If *Conejo* maintained his story with his daughter's life on the line, they would return Emma unharmed to her mother and kill him quickly. Otherwise this was going to be a long drawn out night, the kind of night he loathed.

~

"Told you, my gut instinct was right," Cervera said. He was bent over examining the remains of a skinny tattooed young man, dumped by the roadside on the outskirts of Cancun. The guy's throat had been cleanly slit from side to side through both carotid arteries. It would have been a speedy end but not before he had undergone quite a bit of torture. His throat and chest had what looked like burns, consistent with the marks left by a Taser. Filthy pants covered the guy's groin, but Cervera would bet money on his *cojones* having the same marks.

"You recognize him?" Asked Toledo. He snapped a couple of photos with his camera, while they waited for the coroner to arrive.

"Si, he's one of Fuentes' guys." He pointed at the dead guy's prominent front teeth, "He's the one they call *Conejo*, Rabbit."

"Why do you think his death is connected to the Romanians and the ATM problems?"

"I've been hearing rumblings that the Romanian boss is paying big money to convert Fuentes' foot-soldiers to his crew." Cervera placed his hands on his knees, pushing himself upright. "I think this one got caught."

Toledo stopped taking photos and stared down at the corpse. "Any other clever rumblings from your gut? Like who killed him?" He jibbed.

"Fuentes."

Toledo loudly guffawed.

"Laugh all you want, but I know I'm right."

"How?"

"A Taser is Fuentes favourite tool to encourage a person to talk."

"That's it? That's your proof?" Toledo turned his head sharply to stare at Cervera. "We have both seen the results of Fuentes' handiwork, and this is too clean." He pointed at the body.

"Exactly, I think *Conejo* talked without too much prompting," Cervera said, waggling one hand in a *mas ó menos* gesture, more or less. *Conejo* was a mess, so, yes, he had been tortured but not as much as some of the victims that they had come across in recent years.

Cervera crossed one arm across his sizeable stomach and propped his chin on the other hand. "This still gets the point across to the rest of his crew. Double-cross me and will you die. But, give me information about the rivals and you will die quickly."

"*En serio,*" Toledo snorted. "You want me to believe he has a conscience?"

"Not a conscience, but a code of ethics."

"Marco, Marco, Marco," Toledo shook his head, "Over the years you've had some really weird ideas. But this new ... *theory* ... is a pile of horseshit."

"We'll see," Cervera answered. "We'll see.

Chapter 14

April 25th Isla Mujeres

Jessica liberally soaped her body as she sang loudly and off-key to a favourite Zac Brown Band tune playing on iTunes, "Toes in the water, ass in the sand, not a worry in the world, cold beer in my hand, life is good today. Life is good today!"

Sparky lay on the bathroom floor keeping a watchful eye on her. She poked her head through the entrance of the tiled-shower cubicle, "Hey, bud, are you worried that I might escape for a drive without you? Or you don't like my singing?"

He wagged in response to the second question. His tail reminded her of the baby-bottle brush she had recently bought, for cleaning the red wine stains from the inside of her goblets; short, white and bristly.

"Ooooh, that means you don't like my singing. Me either, it sucks." She laughed then turned off the shower and stepped onto the tile floor, reaching for a towel. Her bath towels were air-dried on an outdoor clothesline and she liked their rough feel as she briskly rubbed her skin.

Sparky's head swung around, looking towards her front door.

She watched his face as she stepped into her thong, and fastened her bra. "Is someone here, Sparky?"

He got up to investigate whatever had caught his attention while she tossed on a pair of shorts and a top, then padded barefoot after him. He was sniffing an envelope that was poked under the door. She picked it up, turned in over and saw her name was printed on the front. She held it up to the light, a note was tucked inside. Intrigued she lifted the flap and removed the piece of paper.

She unconsciously read it aloud, "Dear Jessica, I know you are probably still angry with me, but I would really like to apologize in person. I had no idea who Kirk Patterson was wanted for murder in the US. I certainly wouldn't have done anything to harm either Yasmin or you. Would you meet me today for a cup of coffee? Around ten o'clock at Rooster on the Go?" It was signed by Ryan Whitecross.

"Like hell I will! You sniveling little shit," She muttered. Crumpling the paper, she tossed it into her garbage can. Still stewing over the note, she banged around in her kitchen for a few minutes, organizing a pot of coffee but didn't switch it on. "Why should I listen to him whine about poor him, he was misled by that bad old Kirk Patterson?" She said looking at Sparky for support.

She sighed. "At times I really miss having a roommate who can talk."

She checked the time on her phone. Nine-thirty, time enough to give her pooch a pee break and still get there by ten. She picked up Sparky's leash and her keys. "Dammit! Why doesn't he just leave me alone?"

Swiping the screen on her phone she found Diego's number and while listened to it ring, held Sparky's harness for him to step into. Her call went to voicemail,

"Hi Diego, this is Jessica. I'm meeting Ryan Whitecross at Rooster on the Go at ten. He says he wants to apologize. I am beyond thrilled," She said with a heavy dose of snark in her voice, "Anyway, I just thought I should tell someone ... just in case.

"Okay, Sparky. Let's go and get this over with."

~

Jockeying *Frita Bandita* into a tight parking space Jessica turned off the ignition, and untied the lead. They stepped out of the golf cart and onto the sidewalk.

"Stay, I'll see if Ryan is here." She pointed at a shady spot under a table. Sparky sat and watched her disappear into the coffee shop. "He's not here yet," She said as she returned to her vehicle and pulled out a yellow plastic bowl and a bottle of water that she had brought for him. She poured a little water into the dish and set it in front of him.

He ignored it.

Jessica popped back inside to pick up the grande latte that she had ordered and sat in a chair near Sparky. "Ten minutes. If he isn't here in ten minutes, we're outta here."

"Jessica!" Shouted a familiar voice.

"Oh, damn. He showed up," She muttered. She briefly lifted one hand in a laconic greeting. "Hi."

"Hola, Jessica. Thank you so much for coming."

"Sure." She glanced at him. He looked the same; blonde hair, green eyes and a really fit body.

"I was going to buy your coffee. I'll just get mine. Would you like a muffin or a cookie to go with your coffee?"

"No thanks, I don't have a lot of time. I have to work today." She didn't have to be at the *Loco Lobo* until four in the afternoon, but he wouldn't remember what time she normally started work.

"Oh, yes, of course," He stuttered, "Give me five minutes to get a coffee."

"Yep."

As he rushed inside to order his coffee, Jessica looked at Sparky and rolled her eyes. She was pretty sure her dog was laughing at her.

Too soon Ryan was back with his coffee, and pulled up a chair at her table.

Jessica noticed Sparky sniff Ryan's feet. His tail flicked once in a disinterested greeting, then he rested his head on his paws. *Interesting.* He had met the man a couple of times during her treasure hunting fiasco but the dog and man typically ignored each other. Most people, when confronted with a friendly tail-wagging dog, smiled and asked if it was okay to pat Sparky, exclaiming, *oh, isn't he adorable*?

Maybe she should have paid closer attention to Sparky's reaction.

"Why are you back on Isla?" She asked Whitecross. She had no patience for superficial small talk, she just wanted to get this over with.

"I ... well, I didn't like how things ended between us. I wanted to make amends."

"Ryan, we had sex a couple of times. That's all it was — sex." *And, it had been entertaining*, she mused, *until she discovered what he and Patterson were up to.*

"I think it could have developed into a deeper more meaningful relationship if you had let me explain."

Instead of telling him what a completely brainless a-hole she thought he was to be taken in by a manipulative killer, she smiled coldly and said, "Ryan, it was sex. It was fun. And I am not interested in a deeper, more meaningful relationship with you." She started to stand.

He clasped her arm, "Wait, please."

"Don't," She snarled as she flung her arm up and away from her body, dislodging his grip.

"I'm sorry, I'm really sorry," His open hands popped up to his shoulders, in an attempt ward off her anger. "Please, just let me explain. Then if you are still angry, I'll leave you alone."

She stared down at him, "I'm listening."

Ryan's face registered resignation. He had finally realized she wasn't going to sit and share a friendly chat. "Okay. I admit I was a sucker for believing Patterson when he said he wanted to *help* you and Yasmin find the pirate's cache. I also had no idea that he had tried to break into Yasmin's home and intended to rape her. I just thought he was someone to hang out with, to chase chicks, and drink a few beers while I was on vacation." He sighed. "I am very sorry for everything that happened."

"Apology accepted." She bent to retrieve the dog dish, emptied the water into a nearby planter and then tugged on his lead, "Come on boy. Let's go."

She could feel Ryan's reproachful eyes follow her as she drove away.

Chapter 15

April 26th Isla Mujeres

Fuentes shifted his body in his office chair; an erection tightening his pants made him uncomfortably aware that his obsession with Jessica was becoming a liability. He held his phone in his hand, staring again at the screensaver.

Pinche pendejo! Maddened by his irrational obsession he leapt up, jerked at his underwear and strode to the bathroom. He glared at his image in the mirror.

He was certain she wouldn't recognize him. The only time she had a good look at him was when he was pretending to be a waiter at the Mendoza-Medina wedding reception. He had been clean shaven and had let his hair grow longer. After his botched attempts to kill her, he had reverted to tightly shorn hair and a luxurious moustache.

If he left his bodyguards and Rodriquez behind, he could travel incognito to the island. Then pay her a visit. A nice long visit. But that would only be a temporary solution. As soon as his satisfaction had worn off, he would crave more.

His other problem was the freaking mutt. It would remember his scent, and attack him. He could poison the dog.

Or, he could order his crew to kidnap her and keep her locked in his compound.

He slammed his palm against the mirror, almost breaking the glass. "Get a grip, the worldwide media would go nuts if a beautiful blonde *gringa* went missing in Mexico," He muttered at his image. "We sure as hell don't want to frighten our best customers, the tourists."

He also couldn't let anyone know of his fixation with this woman. She was a weakness to be exploited by underlings hoping to topple him, or by enemies wanting his territory.

Plus, he still had to deal with Dacey Uicab, the ATM technician who was working for the Romanians. By now he had probably noticed that his co-worker Lionel Hau hadn't been at work recently. Uicab needed to be grabbed before he scuttled into hiding like a cockroach avoiding a bright light.

Fuentes stomped over to his office door and jerked it open. "Rodriquez. Get in here," He bellowed.

"Si, *Don* Fuentes," Rodriquez replied as his footsteps thudded along the corridor.

Before his lieutenant had reached the office door, Fuentes barked at him, "Pick up that technician, Uicab. I want to have a little chat with him." Fuentes flapped a hand, dismissing Rodriquez.

"Claro, Jefe," Rodriquez replied, turning on his heels and striding back with way he had come.

Fuentes banged the door shut and ran a hand over his shorn hair. His mouth quirked into a rictus of a smile. *Now, I get why cartel bosses are psychotic killers. Always under enormous stress and can't trust anyone, it's enough to make anyone nuts.*

~

Diego's long muscular legs stretched towards the centre of their small family kitchen. His hands behind his head, he leaned against the back of the chair. "Tell me again why you met up with Whitecross," He said, with a note of incredulity.

Cristina's hands were busy with washing up their lunch dishes. She looked at Jessica over one shoulder, "I thought you hated him," She said.

"Hate. That a strong word. I hated that evil bastard Kirk Patterson. I intensely dislike Ryan Whitecross." Jessica reached for a tea towel. She dried and stacked the clean dishes on the counter top. This kitchen was as familiar to her as hers was, having enjoyed many delicious meals with her friends and their four active youngsters.

"So why meet up with him?" Diego asked.

"Oh hell, I don't know." She flipped her long blonde plait over one shoulder and curbed her urge to fiddle with the end. It was a childhood habit that annoyed her mother, but one that she reverted to when feeling insecure. "My Canadian politeness? Curiosity about what he would say? I have no clue."

"What did he say?" Cristina probed.

"He was sorry. He didn't know Kirk Patterson very well. He was just a buddy to hang out with ... blah, blah, blah."

"And what did you say?" Asked Diego. He leaned forward and wiggled his fingers at Sparky, signalling that he was willing to give him a pat and a butt-scratch. He obliged and leaned into Diego's hand. "That feels good, doesn't it boy?"

Jessica snorted a laugh, "I feel like a tennis ball. First Diego lobs a question, and then Cristina, then Diego again."

"Then it's my turn," Cristina said, "So, what did you say?"

Watching Diego and Sparky contentedly interact Jessica answered Cristina, "I said, apology accepted. Goodbye."

"If he calls again, will you see him?" Cristina asked. She reached for a pot and started scouring the inside with a green scrubby.

"No, I still intensely dislike Whitecross." She stopped drying, and stretched over Cristina's head to place the stack of colourful terracotta plates on a sturdy wooden shelf.

"Will he be leaving the island?"

"I have no idea and don't care, as long as he stays out of my face."

"It seems a bit odd that he came back to the island to apologize, when he could have just sent you a message via any of your social media accounts," Diego said, as he stood up and enfolded Cristina in an embrace. He kissed the back of her neck. "Any chance of another cup of coffee, *mi amor*?"

Jessica smiled as Cristina leaned back and momentarily closed her eyes. She was obviously savouring the feel of Diego's bunched muscles and the heat radiating through his t-shirt. "Mmmm," She dried her hands and tilted her face up. "But it will cost you a kiss."

He bent his head and kissed her long and thoroughly.

Jessica laughed, "Geez, will you just get a room?" She wasn't jealous, but she was a little envious of their very deep and visible love.

Diego ignored Jessica, kissing Cristina again while amorously running his hands over his wife's voluptuous curves. When their lips disengaged for the second time, Diego bounced his eyebrows at Jessica in an amusingly familiar gesture. "You're just jealous." He quipped.

"Yep, I am. Now stop all that mushy stuff in front of your sex-deprived friend."

"What happened to you and Luis?" Cristina asked. She removed the scrunchie that held her dark tresses in a long ponytail and scrapped back her hair. Satisfied with the results, she secured her mane with the hair ornament and began to organize another pot of coffee.

"Nothing really, we just lost interest in each other." We're still friendly, we're just not feeling the spark anymore." Jessica chewed on her bottom lip. She couldn't put it into words, but something had dramatically changed after the two attempts on her life. Her world had suddenly come into sharper focus. If she was honest with herself, she was a bit bored with her life.

Her sense of boredom was damn ironic considering the last two and a half years had been one adventure after another. But something was missing in her life, and she wasn't sure what the *something* was – yet.

"I'm sorry, what did you say?" Jessica pulled herself back from her reverie.

"Mas café?" Cristina pointed at the aromatic brew burbling into the carafe.

"Si, por favor." Jessica turned and opened the refrigerator door, reaching for the open container of skimmed milk.

Chapter 16

April 27th Isla Mujeres

"Well, look what the cat dragged in." Jessica teased as she saw Carlos and Yasmin arrive at the restaurant holding hands.

Carlos tipped a tight-lipped smile at her, then glanced towards the day-time bartender, "Isabela, can you stay a little longer? I need a few minutes with Yasmin and Jessica."

"*Por supuesto, no hay problema*," Isabela responded.

Jessica's eyebrows crunched together as she studied his resolute expression. Carlos motioned to his office and she followed them, closing the door behind her. "Is there problem, boss?"

"Yes," He said. He pulled the chair out from behind his desk and settled into it, then looked at Jessica.

"Okay," She replied tentatively. "So, what's wrong?"

"We are going to close the *Loco Lobo*."

Jessica's stomach did a little flip. Changes were unsettling, but in a good way. Maybe this was her clue to do something different with her life. Whatever happened, Sparky would be part of her future plans.

"I'm sorry to hear that," She said, "I thought the *Loco Lobo* was very successful."

Yasmin smiled at her friend's uncertain expression. "He's messing with you, Jess. We want to move the restaurant to a beachfront location."

"Damn it, you had me going there," Jessica laughed. "Where?"

"We can't be specific until we sort out a few things. There's a problem with the title," Carlos answered, his face relaxing into a crooked grin.

"Yeah, that's not a big surprise," Jessica said with a so-what shrug of one shoulder. "Almost every purchase, that I know about, has been complicated."

Carlos nodded, "Si, many of the original families don't have the legal title even though their ancestors have lived on the land for a hundred years or more."

"Inheriting the land can create a legal mess," Yasmin interjected. "In this case three of the siblings want to sell the property and two don't."

"It will take a bit of time and money but we'll get it sorted out," Carlos said. "I have a good *notario* working on it."

"Luis?" Asked Jessica. She momentarily regretted that she and Luis Aguilar had drifted apart. He was fun to be with and so good in bed.

"Si, he's smart and more importantly, honest. He'll work it out with the siblings."

"And then you have to sort it out with the bureaucrats." Jessica said, as she rubbed her thumb and two fingers together in the sign for a bribe.

"Si, *mordidita*, a little bite," Yasmin agreed.

"Will you keep the same name?" Jessica asked.

"Absolutely!" Yasmin answered. "We have a loyal customer base, but we can ramp up the fun factor with live music in the late afternoon, early evenings."

Carlos tipped his head considering Jessica's question, "Do you have a different idea, Jess?"

"Yes, a pirate-themed restaurant. Call it *The Treasure Trove*, or *A Pirate's Delight*. You could decorate the building to resemble a pirate's ship, with netting, and riggings, and piles of loot. Or call it *The Hacienda Hideaway* and make it look like pirate Mundaca's house, dark timbers and rough plaster walls with iron lanterns." Her hands flapped expressively as she explained her idea, "And you could have one of those realistic pirate statues standing guard at the door."

"But there is already a pirate-themed restaurant on the island," Yasmin interjected, as she discretely moved a half-full beverage container a few inches further away from Jessica's flailing hands.

Jessica waggled her right hand back and forth, "Sort of. It has a pirate-ish name, but as far as I am concerned there's not much in the way of atmosphere."

Yasmin pushed out her bottom lip as she reconsidered her initial objection. "You're right. That one has a very basic ambiance. What do you think, Carlos?"

"I like it a lot, and you ladies can be tavern wenches," He said with a mischievous glint in his eyes.

Jessica shook her head and looked down at her chest, "I have what my grandfather referred to as a pirate's delight.

"Wait a minute. You just suggested that as a name for the new restaurant. Does it have an off-colour double-meaning in English?" Carlos asked.

Jessica grinned at his expression. It was a little payback for the stress he had caused her with his announcement that they were closing the restaurant.

"A pirate's delight is a sunken chest!" Jessica guffawed. "There's not much in the way of wench material on this body. I'd have to stuff my bra with socks."

Yasmin laughed, "Oh god, I remember when you did that for a Halloween party at Villa la Bella. You had a long dark wig, gobs of makeup, and four pairs of socks stuffed in your bra to give you a sexy cleavage. None of the guys recognized you."

"And that confirmed my theory, men check your boobs before looking at your face," Jessica retorted.

"Guilty as charged," Carlos agreed laughing. "I think I was at that same party, but to be honest I didn't know you very well at the time."

"Yes, you were there, ogling my jiggling boobs with the rest of the bug-eyed lechers. I remember very clearly," Jessica replied, a teasing smirk twisted her lips.

"I also remember the year you wore a very sexy, skin-tight Spiderman suit – backwards," Carlos retorted with mischief in his eyes. "If I remember correctly it had something to do with drinking a couple of glasses of vino before you got dressed."

"Oh, my God. I had forgotten that." Jessica and Yasmin collapsed in giggles. "I clearly remember a woman coming up to me at the party and saying, 'Jessica, are you trying to make a statement with that costume?' And I asked her why? 'Because, honey, you have it on backwards.'"

"It was pretty funny," Yasmin agreed, wiping her eyes.

"I struggled by myself in their tiny, hot, poolside bathroom for fifteen minutes. I had to peel the suit off, then get it the right way around and pull it back over my sweaty body," Jessica reminisced with laughter in her voice. "I finally had to find someone to pull the zipper all the way up the back for me."

"That was me," Yasmin declared. "I zipped you up."

"Was that the year Elmo was my date?" Jessica asked. "Or Mickey Mouse?"

"I honestly don't remember, I'd have to look at the photographs again," Yasmin said. "I really miss those Halloween parties."

"Me, too, but seriously, what do you think of my pirate idea?" Jessica asked.

Carlos and Yasmin exchanged looks and she answered. "It's worth thinking about, maybe get a rough design drawn up. See what the cost would be."

"We're starting from scratch on this Jess. We don't own this building," He said, lifting his right hand to indicate the premises of the *Loco Lobo*, "We just lease it. And we had a lot of repairs after Hurricane Pablo. Money will be very tight for us, but I like your idea."

"A bit of uncertainty is good for your brain," Jessica countered. "It keeps your blood pumping and your grey cells working, while you figure out a solution." She grinned to herself. *Maybe you should follow your own advice.*

Chapter 17

April 27th Cancun

Cervera extracted a wallet from the dead man's back pocket using the tip of his thumb and forefinger. He riffled through identification and held up a business card with a name matching a driver's licence.

"Dacey Uicab Che," He said pronouncing the complete name. "Well, well, he's a technician for the company that services a number of the bank ATMs." Cervera flicked the edge of the card with his thumb nail, "I wonder which of the players he annoyed – our local bad-guy Fuentes or the Romanians."

Walking carefully around the man Toledo snapped photos using his phone, "Did you call the meat wagon?" He asked.

"Si, the coroner is on the way." Cervera held the business card with two fingers while he punched in the main phone number and listened to it ring.

"Looks dead to me," Toledo said, pointing at the mess that would have been the man's head.

"Claro," Cervera scanned the area. Six uniformed officers were spaced at intervals, keeping looky-loos away. "Who's that?" He poked his chin in the direction of a nearby police cruiser. A tiny beribboned Schnauzer was incongruously tucked between the owner's muscular chest and forearm like a stuffed toy being cradled by a giant.

"Must be the dog-walker who found the body and called it in."

Taller by at least a head than Cervera, the man leaned against a police cruiser waiting for someone to take his statement. Wiping the sweat from his eyes, he appeared to be regretting his civil-minded phone call.

Cervera indicated that he had heard but he was paying attention to the recording, then he punched a key and waited. "Bueno," He said when the call was finally answered. "This is Detective Marco Cervera of the State Police Homicide Department. I need to speak to your manager." He studied the ruined body while he waited for the call to be transferred.

"Bueno. This is Leoncio Pastrana, I am the vice-president. How can I help you?"

"Do you have an employee by the name of Dacey Uicab Che, who is a service technician?"

"This is a large company. I couldn't possibly know all the names of our employees. I will transfer you to our Human Resources Department," The man snipped.

"Momentito!" Cervera commanded.

"Now what?"

"You might want to ask *why* a homicide detective is calling."

"Claro," Pastrana peevishly acknowledged. "Why are you calling?"

"A man we believe was your employee has been murdered."

"Again, that is nothing to do with me. I'll transfer you now."

"*Pinche pendejo*!" Muttered Cervera as he heard his call being transferred to another number. He saw the coroner walk towards the body and set her bag on the ground. He nodded a friendly greeting to her.

"Bueno." Another voice answered.

""This is Detective Marco Cervera of the State Police Homicide Department. Who am I speaking to?" Cervera asked, concentrating on the phone conversation while keeping an eye on the doctor as she started her examination.

"This is Paola Che, I am the director of human resources."

Cervera glanced again at the card in his hand, Che. She could possibly be a relative of the dead man. He introduced himself, then asked, "Are you related to Dacey Uicab Che?"

"Si," she replied warily. "He is my cousin on my mother's side. Why?"

He glanced at his watch, "My partner Detective Toledo and I will be at your office in twenty minutes."

"Why? What's happened?"

"We'll explain when we see you." He disconnected before the woman could lob anymore anxious questions at him.

Toledo cast a questioning glace at his partner.

"The Human Resources Director is a cousin to our dead guy. I want to tell her in person, so that I can see her reaction." He turned to the coroner, "Buen día, Doctora."

"Buenos días, Marco. Cómo estás?"

"Bien, bien. Todo bien. Gracias. Y tu?"

"Todo bien. Who do we have here?" She asked.

Toledo gave her a quick rundown on what they knew so far. Cervera explained he needed to inform a relative where Uicab worked of his death and get more information.

"Are we done here Doctora?" Toledo asked.

"Si, I will have the autopsy report for you by tomorrow."

~

Cervera hefted his bulk behind the steering wheel of their unmarked cruiser, while Toledo settled himself in the passenger seat. Neither man bothered with the seatbelts. It was ironic that the policía in Cancun weren't required to use the devices, but the taxi drivers were. Nabbing a cab driver who wasn't wearing a seat belt was a decent source of income for the traffic constables. The result was most taxi drivers pulled the seatbelt across their torso, but didn't click the strap into the lock. It was an amusing battle between the two *machismo* vocations.

You can't tell me what to do!

Oh, yes, I can.

Less amusing was their interview with Paola Che, the director of human resources for the ATM service company. When they notified her of her cousin's death, she expressed distress but at the same time she was nervous and unhelpful. Cervera suspected she was involved in, or knew about, whatever led to her cousin's death.

Che gave them the addresses and phone numbers for his wife and his parents. That was their next task a NOK, the next of kin notification. It was the part of the job that every police officer hated, that and having to ask a family member to formally identify the body.

In the case of Dacey Uicab Che, Cervera hoped the man had tattoos or distinguishing marks on his body because his head and face were ruined. No family member should have that vision as the last memory of their loved one.

~

"Another technician is dead?" Spittle flew from the mouth of Adrian Bortos. Gone was his mild-mannered, average-guy appearance. In its place was a contorted face, flushed purple with rage.

A large heavy object sailed past the head of Emanoil Bilea and smashed against the wall behind him. Bilea held himself steady. Showing fear would escalate Bortos' tantrum.

"Yes, boss. Fuentes is housecleaning," Bilea responded.

"Recruit more!"

"We are trying but everyone is terrified of Fuentes."

"Then demonstrate that they should be more afraid of me."

"Yes, boss," Bilea replied. He and Pirjol had been ruthless in their most recent attempts at recruiting, but so far everyone had resisted. One man finally admitted that all of the service technicians had received graphic photographs of what had happened to Dacey Uicab. They were so shocked that many had quietly abandoned their jobs and moved their families to other cities.

Their employer was panicking. New employees were rushed through a basic maintenance program for the thousands of ATMs crammed into the lucrative hotel zone, and outlying areas such as Isla Mujeres, Playa del Carmen, and Cozumel. Even some of the low-level office managers were being forced to help out.

Privately, Bilea thought their terror tactics were creating chaos and decreasing their revenue, but he valued his life too much to openly disagree with his boss. He also knew that Fuentes had uncovered their names; Bortos, Pirjol, and himself.

That bit of information he would keep to himself otherwise he and Pirjol would be disposed of to sever ties between them and Bortos. It might be time to cut and run. Empty his bank accounts and assume a new identity – far, far away from this lunatic.

Bortos drummed his fingers on his desk. "Get a job," He ordered.

Bilea quietly sucked in his breath, "I'm sorry boss, I don't understand. Are you firing me?" If Bortos wanted him gone, he would be dead before he reached the front door.

"No. You and Pirjol will get a job with the ATM service company. You will be my inside guys."

"But, we're not Mexican, boss."

"You are both fluent in English and Spanish," Bortos stared flat-eyed at his subordinate. "Two days and I will have American passports and work permits in your names. Then both of you will start working for the company. Bribe or coerce the person doing the hiring if necessary."

Bilea thought about that for a minute. It could work. He already had a connection with Paola Che the director of human resources. In exchange for an occasional bit of mediocre sex, a regular supply of drugs and a little cash she gave him the names and phone numbers for the other technicians, including her now very dead cousin Dacey. Bortos didn't need to know about the relationship.

"Okay, boss. Whatever you need, we'll do it."

"Yes, you will," Bortos stated.

Chapter 18

May 3rd Isla Mujeres

He had a vague idea of where she lived and the locals were happy to help Jessica's pleasant friend. One teenage boy gave him detailed directions to the house of the pretty blonde *gringa* who owned the famous pooch Sparky. He wasn't sure who the kid was more enamoured with, Jessica or her mongrel.

He pulled into a shady spot a few doors away from her house, and switched off the motorcycle engine. He left his full-face helmet in place. It was hot and uncomfortable but he needed it as a disguise.

~

Sparky lay at Jessica's feet, panting in the sunshine. "For a Mexi-mutt you sure don't like the heat." Jessica said as she lightly rubbed his spotted tummy.

His belly was sparsely covered by straight white fur, contrasting with the thick curly fleece on his shoulders and rump. He was a tweedy mix of grey and white with two large chocolate brown spots; one on his left side, and one centred on his butt like a target. His front feet were larger than his back feet, and frequently when he sat, they were turned splayed at a forty-five-degree angle. The dark racoon mask that surrounded his inquisitive brown eyes matched the colour of his silky ears.

Jessica grinned, remembering the comment from a visiting Canadian veterinarian, *Holy Cow, this dog is hung*. Sparky was rather well-endowed, especially for a short-legged neutered male, and when anyone asked her what type of breed he was, her standard reply was pure-bred Mexican low-rider. A mutt.

Sparky flapped his tail, then reluctantly stood up and moved away from her soothing touch. He flopped on his side in the shade.

Warmed by the late morning sun and a fresh cup of hot coffee Jessica relaxed back into the Adirondack-style chair on her tiny back patio.

Today was the Day of the Flowery Cross in Mexico, a celebration for construction workers particularly the stone masons. She idly watched the workers in the unfinished interior of a new building that was squashed onto the adjoining lot and pushed up against her landlord's back fence.

One of the workers was carefully decorating a cross made from pieces of wood scavenged from the work-site. The broad-shouldered man wound multiple pieces of crepe paper around the icon. His large work-calloused hands created a beautiful pattern of colours: red, green, yellow, orange and blue. As a finishing touch, he secured bright flowers on the pieces of wood. The effect was simple and stunningly beautiful.

A few minutes later she could see the labourers tote the man-sized cross to the highest point on the building. One well-padded young guy inched on his stomach to the edge of the domed roof to place the icon in exactly the right spot.

"Yeah, I wouldn't want to be him," She said, to Sparky who barely acknowledged her comment. "At least he did it before drinking the free beer."

Once the cross was secured in place Jessica saw the men bow their heads. The first time she had seen this celebration she had asked Diego what it was all about. He had said they were praying for safety on the job site and prosperity for the coming year.

Then it was time for the crew to relax and celebrate with food and beer supplied by their boss and the owner of the building.

"It's going to get a bit noisy, little man." She said, moving off the chair and opening her screen door. "Want to go for a ride?"

Sparky leapt up and barged past her legs.

"So, I guess that's a yes," She said as she shut and locked her door.

Out on the street she climbed into the cart. She secured Sparky in his harness and tied his leash around the steering column. "Okay, where do you want to go?"

Sparky turned and looked at her as if to say, *you're driving, not me.*

Jessica glanced over her shoulder to check for traffic before she pulled out into the narrow street. A couple of houses away a man wearing jeans, a long-sleeved shirt, riding gloves and a full-face helmet sat on a large black motorbike.

That's odd. That type of helmet was too hot for this climate, especially one that was all black and looked like something Darth Vader would choose. She knew one islander who liked to wear a full-face helmet and this wasn't him. He had a white helmet and rode a red motorbike, plus he knew Jessica and would have waved a friendly greeting.

When she studied the man, he seemed to sense her unease and turned his head sideways in a less threatening posture.

Driving away from her casa a spike of apprehension travelled up her spine, causing the tiny hairs at the back of her neck to lift. She glanced at Sparky but he was oblivious to her concern and happily strained against the harness, leaning out to feel the breeze on his face.

"Probably just my overactive imagination," She muttered glancing nervously in the rear-view mirror. The man hadn't moved.

She shrugged, *maybe he's waiting for a friend*.

~

"You and I are going to get to know each other so much better." The man whispered as she drove away. He knew from past experiences the anticipation was far more enjoyable then the act.

He scrutinized the neighbourhood. The construction workers were engaged with their celebration. The street contained numerous parked motos and vehicles, but no people. Today was a school vacation day and the kids were probably sleeping or glued to whatever handheld electronic device they owned. Their parents were either at work or inside preparing the mid-day meal. He confidently strode towards her casa.

He pulled a long slender tool out of his side pocket and raked the tumbler of the front door lock. In less than a minute he was inside. "You really need to upgrade your locks," He murmured, as he shut the door. Feeling confident that she would avoid returning home until she thought the construction crew had finished their fiesta, he leisurely began to inspect her dwelling. Decorated in vibrant tropical hues the living area looked comfortable and uncluttered. He liked it, not that it mattered.

In the bathroom were the usual array of shampoos, conditioners, and body washes. The basket of toiletries revealed that she was taking oral contraceptives. Good. He slid one of the pills into his pocket. He would ensure he had a supply of the same brand on hand.

Next he headed to her bedroom, opening drawers and fingering her clothing. It was all pretty standard choices for a nearly-thirty single woman living in the tropics. She has an assortment of t-shirts and shorts, a few summery dresses, a light jacket, and a stack of colourful sandals. One drawer contained a collection of lacy bras and thongs. He caressed one of the skimpy bits of turquoise lace and the matching bra. *She would look stunning in this,* he mused as he carefully folded the items and pushed them into a pocket.

In a basket on top of the dresser was a collection of jewelry, intended to add a bit of sex appeal for a date night. His lips twitched as he poked at the assortment of inexpensive baubles. He would prefer to drape her naked body with real gemstones.

He exited the house quicker than he had entered, not stopping to re-engage the lock. The thought of her uncertainty when she discovered her unlocked door made his gut tingle with anticipation.

Chapter 19

May 3rd Isla Mujeres

Sparky stood up and rested his chin on the edge of her chair, giving her the full, sad-eye treatment. *Don't you love me anymore?*

Jessica snorted with laughter, "You're a manipulative little devil."

She had driven Sparky to his favourite swimming spot, then walked him a bit until he dried off, and finally settled down at a sidewalk cafe with a large latte and her reader. She quickly became immersed in the exciting mystery set in Acapulco. It was the newest novel in the Emilia Cruz series written by Carmen Amato.

Although she was enjoying the book, she was also peripherally aware of Sparky's restive behaviour. He sighed and shifted positions every fifteen minutes just to remind her that he was feeling neglected and bored. Unappreciated.

She tipped back the last drop of her latte and gathered up her insulated coffee mug, Kindle reader, and phone. "Alright let's go home."

"*Arriba*!" Jessica said.

"Passenger," She added, telling him to get over to his own side and move his fuzzy butt away from the gas and brake pedals.

The typically congested afternoon traffic in Centro was going to make her dentist rich. She clamped her jaw, and ground her teeth to keep from yelling at the drivers who blocked traffic while posing for the perfect selfie-smile.

At times like this she really wished she had a loud Ooga-horn to remind them to move over. *Frida Bandita* originally had a horn but with the salt and humidity it lasted about six months before turning into a tangle of corroded wires and metal bits.

Twenty minutes later Jessica maneuvered her little vehicle into a tiny parking spot in front of her house.

Sparky strained against his leash as he sniffed the air and the ridge of course hair running along his spine became more visible.

"What's up, bud?" She untied him from the cart, but held his leash in her hand. He towed her across the sidewalk towards her *casa*.

A rumble started in his chest.

Jessica looked up and down the street, searching for the cause of Sparky's agitation. Nothing looked out of place. She scrutinized her front door. It didn't seem to be fully closed. She touched the handle and the door eased open.

"Shit! That was locked." She forcefully hauled Sparky away from her front entrance and headed towards her neighbours' house. "Enrique! Rosa! Are you home?" She hollered as she raised her fist to knock on their door.

"Si, momentito," Enrique Castillo called from behind the door. A few seconds later his round smiling face appeared followed by his large stomach, and his boxy physique. "Yessica, so nice to see you," He said reaching to give her a hug and buss on the cheek.

"Hola Enrique," She replied a touch impatiently.

He pulled back; his face creased with uncertainty.

"*Lo siento*, amigo, I have a problem." She was too agitated to share in the affectionate and lengthy greeting expected between friends.

Enrique flapped a hand, "*No hay problema*." He appeared to be willing to forgive her unexpected lack of good manners. "What's wrong?" He asked.

"Sparky and I were out for a few hours. When I came home, I discovered my front door was unlocked."

"Are you sure you locked it?" He asked with a cheeky grin.

"Positive," Jessica answered. "It opened when I touched the handle and Sparky started growling."

"*Claro*, I'll get my son's baseball bat then we'll have a look." He disappeared for a few minutes, then reappeared toting an aluminum bat in one hand. "*Listo*, I'm ready."

"Should I call the police?"

"Why? I told Rosa what we are doing," Enrique said, referring to his wife. "If there is a problem, she's scarier than the policía."

Jessica quirked a knowing grin at her friend. Rosa was a beautiful and diminutive woman with a quick temper. Echoing through the adjoining concrete walls Jessica had on numerous occasions heard Rosa ripping into Enrique for his excessive consumption of *cerveza* on weekends. *Yep, she could be scary.*

Crossing in a few steps to Jessica's front door, Enrique lifted the bat and gently pushed the door wide open. "Policía!" He yelled into the silent house.

Wrapping the excess length of Sparky's lead around her fist Jessica held him beside her leg. She could better control his considerable strength by keeping him on a short leash. His chest vibrated with a deep growl. It was the sound that he made when he recognized the scent of whomever had been at her house, and he didn't like the person.

"Easy, Sparks," She said, using one of his many nicknames.

"Let him off the leash. He'll let us know if anyone is inside." Enrique suggested.

"I'm worried about him being kicked or stabbed."

"Okay then, I'll go first," He said half-heartedly.

"We'll go together," Jessica said, realizing Enrique was nervous. "I have a back door, so the intruder has probably already gone."

He pushed the bat against the door and tried to peer through the crack to see if a bad guy was hiding in behind. Then he craned his neck forward trying to see into her living area.

She couldn't embarrass her friend further by pressuring him to enter her house. Sparky would have to go first. She reluctantly bent to undo his leash and whispered, "Be careful little man, you are my best friend."

He surged around Enrique and barked loudly several times, then he was silent.

"Sparky?" Jessica called. "Sparky *ven aca*," she said in Spanish. When he didn't respond she yelled, "Sparky! Come here!" She pushed past her neighbour.

Enrique followed her with the bat held high, ready to strike at an intruder.

"Sparky," Jessica said, shaking her head. Oblivious to her agitation he was intently sniffing a path through her house.

"You scared me, sweetie."

He ignored her.

Jessica studied Sparky as he carefully followed a trail from her living area through a circuit of the tiny bathroom, and then into her bedroom. She had a second smaller bedroom that was mainly for storage of seldom used items, but he by-passed that room entirely heading straight for her dresser. When he stood on his back legs and pawed at one drawer Jessica could feel a tide of anger flow along her spine and crash into her brain. She nudged the dog aside and opened the drawer.

"*Pinche pendejo bandido*!" She yelled, startling Enrique.

"What's wrong, Yessica?"

Oblivious to his blushing face she pointed at the frothy pile of lingerie. "Some asshole has been in my house and pawed through my underwear!"

Enrique snapped a quick glance into the drawer, then averted his eyes. "How do you know?"

"Because I am a bit OCD about my clothes," She said.

"OCD?"

"Obsessive Compulsive Disorder, I have a need to keep things organized. My thongs and panties are always folded on one side of the drawer and the bras are neatly stacked in rows on the other side," She explained. "I never leave them in a jumble like this." She pointed at the heap of lingerie.

Enrique bounced another quick glance at Jessica then moved away. "Sparky seems calm now," He said, steering the conversation away from lingerie.

She looked at her little buddy, "Yep, he's satisfied there is no danger but he recognizes the scent. If that *pendejo* comes anywhere near me, Sparky will warn me."

"What do you want to do?"

"Get my locks changed," She answered, "but it's a holiday."

"Not for everyone, only for construction workers and school kids," Enrique replied. "My cousin is a locksmith. Let me call him for you."

Listening to Enrique explain the situation to his cousin she scrutinized her home. Earlier she had taken both her phone and her electronic reader with her plus a bit of cash and her driver's license, so those items were secure. She had a television so old even the most desperate drug addict wouldn't bother taking it. She punched the code on her small safe, and confirmed that her credit card and bank card were still locked inside.

Everything looked fine, except the intruder had violated her personal space and ran his filthy hands through her clothes. She strode into her bedroom and forcefully yanked the drawer out of the dresser and upended the contents into her laundry basket, followed by her t-shirts, shorts and sundresses. She briefly considered washing her sandals in the kitchen sink, but decided that was a bit over-the-top.

Turning around she considered her bed. *Surely, he hadn't?* She pulled the coverlet down and examined the sheets. They looked fine, but the feeling of violation was so strong she angrily removed the sheets, pillow cases, mattress cover and heaped everything on top of her clothes.

Enrique ended his call, "He's on the way Yessica."

Jessica reached to give her neighbour a tight hug and a light kiss on his smooth, round cheek. "*Gracias por tu ayuda, mi amigo*, thank you for your help," She said.

He popped one shoulder in a bashful shrug, "De nada."

Chapter 20

May 3rd Isla Mujeres

"I wonder if the break-in is related to the Cuban girls that we helped a few months ago," Maricruz said, as she idly twirled the stem of her empty wine glass.

Jessica gnawed on the end of her thumb. Her quizzical expression was aimed at Maricruz. "Why would you think that?" She couldn't see any possible connection between helping a group of Cuban teenagers who were destined for the North American sex-trade and someone breaking into her house.

"People-traffickers are ruthless people," Maricruz answered. "Maybe the intruder intended to teach you a lesson for interfering." She reached across the table and rested her long slim fingers on Jessica's hand. Her deep brown eyes conveyed disquiet. "You need to be more careful."

"We both helped the girls. Why wouldn't they harass you too?"

"I live in the Navy compound. I'm harder to get at."

"It was just some sick pervert getting his jollies. I'll be fine, Maricruz," Jessica rested her free hand on top and gave her friend's fingers a light squeeze. "I'm sure it was the guy on the motorcycle," Jessica replied.

"Mas vino, mi amor?" Pedro asked Maricruz as he leaned over to still her restive hand.

"Si, por favor."

Pedro softly bussed a kiss across her lips and refilled her glass. Maricruz gently laid an open palm on his smooth cheek to maintain the contact of his lips a little longer. She lovingly kissed him, winked and took a sip of wine.

Jessica felt a slight twinge of envy. *Why couldn't she find someone who loved her like that?*

The group of friends had gathered at Diego and Cristina's to hear Jessica's story about the break-in. As was their habit everyone contributed food for a group dinner. Jessica didn't like to cook, so her routine assignment was to bring sufficient wine. The four Avalos off-spring had finished their meals and were now playing boisterously in the back yard, while the adults lingered at the table with their drinks and the remnants of a delicious meal. Sparky was napping under Jessica's chair, content to be included in the group.

"Do you think the motorcycle rider could have been Ryan Whitecross?" Yasmin asked.

"I don't know," Jessica unfocussed gaze was aimed at her plate as she re-ran her memories like a video on replay mode. "His skin was covered by clothes. His hair and face were completely concealed by the helmet. Male and trim, is about all I remember. It could have been anyone." She shrugged her shoulders, annoyed that she hadn't studied him more closely.

"I don't think Whitecross would have the balls to do something like this," Carlos said. He propped his chin in one hand, his elbow resting on the table. "But you do seem to attract trouble *mi amiga*." His voice teased, yet his face was tight with concern.

"Why don't you think it could be Ryan?" Yasmin quizzed Carlos.

"He's a follower, not a leader."

"But he's in serious lust over Jessica," Diego added.

"Si, he seems to be, but I just don't see him as being this aggressive." Carlos said.

"Sometimes, it the quiet ones that are more dangerous," Diego argued.

"Verdad, true." Carlos conceded.

"Jessica and Sparky can stay with us for a few days," Cristina said, glancing at her Diego for confirmation.

"You and Sparky are always welcome, Jess," Diego snorted a laugh, "but don't expect any privacy. We have four wild kids and one tiny bathroom. They just barge in if they need to use the toilet."

Jessica chuckled at Diego's description. "Thank you, but I'll be fine. I have Sparky, and Enrique's cousin installed those fancy triple-bolt mortise locks on both of my doors … like the ones you put on your doors, Carlos."

"They're worth the money," Carlos laughed and looked sheepishly at Yasmin. "Discovering Elena, still had the keys to my house after our divorce was a bit unnerving," He said. Yasmin quirked a wry grin at him and winked.

Pedro interjected, "As Carlos said, Jessica, you do attract trouble." He too had a smile on his lips but deep in his eyes she could see his concern.

"Enrique left me his son's baseball bat as a backup to Sparky. Truly, I'll be okay," She protested.

"Really Jess, I would love it if you would stay with us," Cristina placed an arm around her shoulders. "And yes, there is no privacy in our house but the kids love you, we love you. Please stay with us."

"Thank you, Tina, but I want to go home."

"Doesn't it bother you that someone was in your casa?" Cristina asked.

Jessica flapped her hand back and forth in a *más o menos*, more or less, gesture. "What bothers me is the pervert had been pawing through my undies. I took everything, all my bed linens and clothes to the laundry service." The thought of some *pendejo* jerking-off in her bed was repulsive. "Andrea had it ready for me before I came here for dinner. I just have to put the clean sheets on my bed, then I am all set."

With a forced smile Jessica said, "Okay, enough about me. What's new with you Yassy?"

Yasmin glanced at Carlos.

"Sure, tell them," He agreed.

"You know we plan to relocate the restaurant, and perhaps, as Jessica suggested, change it to a pirate-theme. We think," Yasmin paused to sketch the sign of the cross.

Jessica curbed a smile. She knew Yasmin was asking God for good luck with their project.

Yasmin continued, "We think we have the land title straightened out, and can start working on permits for the upgrading the docks and building the new restaurant."

"Awesome!" Jessica saluted Yasmin and Carlos with her wine glass.

"*Felicidades*!" Diego held up his bottle of Sol, "Are you really going to name it the *No Boobs Restaurant*?" He dead-panned.

Sputtering with laughter Jessica sprayed her mouthful of wine across the table. She coughed and thumped one fist on her breastbone trying to clear her windpipe. "I'm sorry, I'm sorry." She wheezed.

"*The No Boobs*?" Pedro asked. His thick eyebrows shot upwards to his non-existent hairline. His eyes bounced from Jessica, to Diego, to Carlos.

"It's a joke," grabbing a piece of paper-towel to wipe up her mess Jessica struggled to speak between giggles. "I suggested the name *A Pirate's Delight* as a joke. My grandfather was born long before sensitivity training. He called a flat-chested woman a pirate's delight because she had a sunken chest — no boobs."

Chapter 21

May 3rd Isla Mujeres

Glancing in her rear-view mirror she could see Pedro's headlights following her. He had insisted that Maricruz and he escort her home. She had grumbled and groused at him, saying she didn't need babysitters, but he wasn't going to be dissuaded. He had maintained a consistent distance behind the golf cart all the way from Diego and Cristina's house to their present location.

"It's nice to be loved, I guess," She muttered grumpily to Sparky, "but I really can look after myself." He leaned companionably against her right shoulder and responded with a sloppy grin that revealed his long velvety tongue. Jessica laughed, "So, who do you agree with? With my babysitters? Or with the person who feeds, walks and loves you?"

He just swished his short wiry tail and gave her bare arm a tentative swipe with his tongue.

"A lick! Wow, you never lick anyone. Thanks, little man, I'm honored." She laughed at the absurdity of her dialogue with Sparky, or maybe it was only a monologue since he wasn't actually saying anything.

The food, wine, and time with close friends had helped to lift her spirits and restore her equilibrium. Diego had a wickedly quick sense of humour. The expression on Pedro's face had been priceless when Diego had asked Carlos about the proposed name for the new restaurant; the *No Boobs*. The laughter and joking had continued while the group cleared the table and tidied the kitchen.

The affectionate and lengthy goodbyes, goodnights, hugs and kisses eventually ended and everyone dispersed, leaving just Jessica and her babysitters headed to the eastern side of the narrow island.

Turning right onto the double-wide *Paseo de Aves*, Jessica eased her *carrito* over a nasty, unmarked tope, a speed bump. When the *tope* was new it had been painted a glaring yellow. As time passed the paint had disappeared, incrementally removed by thousands of tires and now the *tope* was an indiscernible driving hazard.

The treacherous *tope* was very familiar to her, but after dark it was easily forgotten. It was directly in front of a community policing outpost; an unfinished house perched on a dark corner with a pit bull chained to the roof. Until recently the municipal policía had been assigned the task of keeping all the *topes* on the island refreshed with yellow high-visibility paint, but for some reason this one was seldom painted. She undoubtedly was a source of amusement for the officers stationed inside the spooky building. On more than one occasion she had loudly cursed as her ass was jolted off the seat, and another bolt or fastener flew off her *carrito* and rattled onto the ground.

But not tonight. She had enjoyed two or maybe it was three glasses of wine with dinner, and didn't want to draw attention to herself. She quietly drove over the obstacle and continued on her way home. She stopped her vehicle near her front entrance and turned to wave goodnight to Pedro and Maricruz, instead, he parked his Nissan truck and they stepped out.

"I'm good. Go home," Jessica flopped one hand in a half-wave.

"We're already parked," Pedro answered. His classical Mayan features, deep hooded eyes and blade-shaped nose gave him a fearsome expression when he had made up his mind; like now. "We'll check inside your house."

"This is ridiculous," Jessica retorted.

"Just open the door, please." He gave her a stink-eye glare.

Jessica huffed, then inserted her new key and unlocked the door.

Pedro blocked her move to enter the house, "I'll go first," He said. His fishing knife with its wicked-looking blade was gripped in his right hand.

"Ooooh, the big strong man is going to protect weak little me," Jessica simpered.

"Shut up."

Jessica blushed, "Yeah. Sorry." She said and stepped aside. She shortened Sparky's leash, preventing him from rushing inside the house.

Pedro and Maricruz coordinated their search of the one level, two-bedroom house; he checked the left side, she the right side. Maricruz wasn't carrying her military sidearm, but she had combat training. Jessica was quick and tough. Maricruz was faster and meaner.

"All clear, Jess," Pedro called a few minutes later.

"Thank you both, but you can't check my house for me every time I take Sparky out for a pee," Jessica said. She was aiming for a grateful tone but heard a hint of exasperation in her voice. She removed Sparky's harness and unlocked her back door. "Go pee, little man," She pointed at the scruffy patch of grass barely visible in the shadows.

"We understand, honestly we do," Maricruz said, "This guy could have planned a second visit tonight hoping that you wouldn't expect him to return so soon."

Jessica's face contorted in frustration, "I really hate this crap."

"Me too," Maricruz said. She put her arm around Jessica's shoulders and tilted her neck until their heads lightly touched. "I'm spending the night and no arguments from you, mi amiga."

"Okay, I give up," She sighed. "Thank you. Again."

"My pleasure." Maricruz released Jessica, and turned to kiss Pedro, "Goodnight my love. Drive safe."

"Goodnight mi amor, sleep well. Call me if anything happens, and I mean anything." He blew Maricruz a kiss and closed the door behind himself.

Sparky wandered back through the open door, wagging happily. "Are you ready for bed little man?" Jessica asked him. She locked the back door, and the front, then double-checked the windows were secured.

"What can I do to help?" Asked Maricruz.

"Help me put the clean sheets on the bed," Jessica said as she slit open the plastic-wrapped bundle of laundry. She scooped up the pile of lacy lingerie set it aside and lifted the sheets out of the plastic, then her hands stilled. She studied the heap of underwear, mentally cataloguing the items. Cursing, she dropped the sheets and frantically began to paw through the bras and panties.

"Jess, what's wrong?" Maricruz asked.

"Jesus H. Freaking Christ, that pervert took some of my undies!" She yelled.

"Easy, Jess. How can you be sure?"

"Because my favourite turquoise bra and thong are missing!" She shouted. "Freaking pervert!"

Chapter 22

May 4th Isla Mujeres

Pedro swiped the screen on his phone and punched the icon to call Diego. He took a sip of coffee while he waited for his brother-in-law to answer.

"*Que pasa*?" Diego answered.

Pedro swallowed and replied, "Maricruz just called to update me. Last night Jessica figured out the intruder took some of her underwear."

"Really? She's sure?"

"According to Maricruz he took her favourite matching set of, as my mother would say, *delicadas*," Pedro answered. "I want to track down Whitecross and ask him where he was and what he was doing yesterday."

"Do you really think it was him?"

"Not sure," Pedro said, "but Jessica is furious. She didn't sleep a whole lot last night. According to Maricruz, Jessica spent most of the night planning what she was going to do to him if she found him."

"If we get to him first, we might save his life. Is that what you're saying?" Diego's deep laugh boomed through the phone's tiny speaker.

"Not necessarily," Pedro replied. "Because, I want to take him on a free fishing charter and have a little heart-to-heart discussion with him."

"We could use him for shark bait."

"Or try a little old-fashioned keel-hauling," Pedro suggested, referring to a punishment common during the era of sailing ships. A sailor charged with breaking the ship's laws would be thrown overboard on one side of the hull and dragged by a line underneath to the other side often resulting in death by drowning, or head injuries.

"Good idea. Much tidier than cutting him up for bait."

Pedro chuckled. His brother-in-law and he shared an inappropriate sense of humour.

"Alright, let's go save her ass — again," Diego said. "But I want a super-hero cape. A red one. I am feeling very underappreciated."

"In Jessica's opinion, Sparky is the super-hero with the red cape. We're just his minions doing his bidding," Pedro rejoined. "I'll pick you up in ten minutes." He ended the call.

~

Pedro eased his foot off the gas, and gently tapped the brakes. He gave the horn a couple of friendly blips to let Diego know he was outside. Normally he would park and visit with his sister before heading out with Diego but he was restless, needing to do something to help Jessica.

"*Hermanito*," Cristina said as she walked towards his vehicle. Diego trailed behind her. "What's the rush?"

He opened the cab door and quickly hugged his sister, "Sorry, Tina, we need to go."

Diego quietly opened the passenger-side door, swung his long body into the seat and pulled the door shut.

"Don't do anything foolish," She scolded Pedro. Her fists rested on her curvy hips.

Pedro pointed at his chest with a finger, "Me? Cristina. You know me better than that."

Cristina snorted and shook her head. "Your middle name should be *Tonto*, foolish." She rested one hand on his arm, "Whatever you two are up to, please be careful."

"I promise, I will," He said shutting the door to the Nissan. "*Te amo, hermanita.*"

As the two men drove away Diego turned to Pedro, "You know your ass is toast if I get hurt. Right?"

"*Claro que se*. I know exactly what my sister would do to me if anything happens to you, oh, Precious One." Grimacing as if he was in severe pain, he put a protective hand over his groin.

Diego threw back his head and roared with laughter.

One side of Pedro's mouth quirked in a mischievous grin. He loved this man. They had been best friends since they were in diapers. "Where do you want to look for Whitecross?"

"Jessica said he suggested they meet at Rooster's coffee shop. Let's start there."

Pedro flicked on the right turn indicator, and spun the steering wheel to turn north onto Rueda Medina. "Good idea. I could use another coffee."

"What do you think of Carlos and Yasmin moving the restaurant to a marina?"

"I think it's a good business decision. Waterfront restaurants are very popular."

"And, maybe they'd give us a deal on berthing the *Bruja del Mar* at their docks," Diego said, his eyebrows popping up towards his hairline.

"Like friends with benefits?" Asked Pedro.

"Si, I'm good with that," Diego dead-panned. Friends with benefits had an off-colour connotation; sex with no emotional complications.

"*Mira*. Look. We're in luck. There's Whitecross," Pedro said popping his chin in the direction of the café. The American was sitting at an outside table, intently studying his phone while he sipped at a tall beverage container.

Pedro parked the vehicle close to the café, and put the transmission in park. He turned off the ignition and stepped onto the pavement. He heard Diego close the passenger door without his usual forceful slam.

Together they approached Whitecross.

The man lifted his head as if he sensed their presence and flinched like a frightened street-dog.

"Hola, Ryan," Pedro said, lifting his hand in a nonchalant wave. He loosened his clenched jaw muscles and tried to appear friendly.

"Hey, Ryan. *Que pasa*?" Asked Diego in a cheerful we're-all-friends-here tone.

Whitecross blinked rapidly, then glanced left and right. He seemed to be considering his escape options.

Pedro smoothly pulled out a chair on one side and Diego on the other side of Whitecross, effectively blocking his exit routes and pinning him against the outside wall of the café.

"We haven't seen you for awhile. How have you been?" Pedro asked. He rested his massive forearms on the small table, causing it to tilt towards him. The container swayed with the movement, spilling some of the warm milky-brown liquid onto the table.

"Fine. I'm fine, thanks," Whitecross sputtered. He steadied the table with one hand and his coffee with the other.

"Oh, hey, sorry about that." Pedro said, grabbing a handful of tiny serviettes and dabbing at the escaping liquid. "I don't know my own strength sometimes." He smiled a toothy grin.

"No worries. It's fine," Whitecross babbled nervously.

"Jessica said the two of you had a little meeting recently," Diego said. His demeanour morphed from a friendly giant into a concerned friend.

"Yes, we did. I just wanted to say I was sorry."

"The note you shoved under her door seems like an invasion of her privacy," Diego said.

"No, no. That wasn't what I intended," Whitecross said, shaking his head. "I only wanted to make amends and see if we could resume our friendship."

"And how did that go?" Asked Pedro, even though he already knew the answer.

"She wasn't receptive to the idea."

"As in she said no, get lost, don't bother me again. Like that?" Diego probed.

"No, she was polite. She just said apology accepted and left." Whitecross looked like someone had just run over his favourite pet.

"What did you do yesterday?" Diego asked.

Whitecross lifted his head, and gave him a puzzled look. "What do you mean?"

"Exactly what I said. What did you do yesterday?"

"All day?" Whitecross asked.

"Si, all day."

"Pretty much what I do every day. Get up, come here for coffee. Spend a couple of hours on the beach. Eat lunch, swim, eat dinner, hit a bar. Go to bed." Whitecross shrugged, "Why?"

"Someone ransacked Jessica's house yesterday." Diego exaggerated, probing for a reaction.

"What? No, hell no. Not me!" Agitated, Whitecross tried to stand causing the table to rock. With a wall of concrete behind and a wall of muscle on either side of him he couldn't escape. "Seriously, I wouldn't do stuff like that. I'm not a nut-job."

Pedro popped Diego a quick, knowing glance followed by a tiny shake of his head. *He's not the guy.*

Diego got to his feet and straightened his chair, then leaned on the back of it with both hands. He studied Whitecross.

Pedro stood and reached out his muscular hand. He gripped Whitecross' slim shoulder and felt the younger man flinch, "I am so glad we had this little chat," He said, maintaining eye-contact.

"Let's hope we don't have to do this again," Diego added.

The two men turned and strolled towards the Nissan.

"Terrified," Pedro murmured out of the side of his mouth.

"Si, shit-scared," Diego quietly agreed. "I don't think it was him."

Chapter 23

May 5th Isla Mujeres

Bilea hefted the heavy satchel supplied by his new employer. His training had been hurried and basic but he had been told he was now a fully qualified service technician for the various ATMs maintained by the company. Buried under the tools and legitimate card readers there were a handful of the modified models supplied by his real boss, Adrian Bortos.

His first assignment was to visit one of the banks on Isla Mujeres. From his comfortable seat on the upper deck of the passenger ferry he had a fantastic view of the turquoise Caribbean Sea, and the low, sandy island as they approached the docks.

Getting hired as a service technician a couple of days ago had been simple. His contact at the ATM company, Paola Che, wasn't ugly and he knew from previous experience offering her a hit of cocaine would speed up the process. She had what was known as a cocaine sex drive. She craved sex when she was high on coke. Shoving aside a collection of files he had used her office desk to satisfy her hunger. She had confided that she enjoyed the danger of discovery. For him it was a version of the old joke; wham bam, thank you ma'am.

Adjusting her clothes and smoothing her hair Paola had tipped him a lewd smile and said, "Welcome to the company."

Bilea had responded in a convincing manner to her flirting while he filled in the employment forms with what they both knew was fake information and signed a signature that wasn't his. She then briefed him on the time-lock procedures common to most banks. She had also emailed the various companies he would be visiting with a copy of his photo ID and his fake name.

Now, two days later he was a certified ATM technician headed to Isla Mujeres. The big blue and yellow passenger boat smoothly settled at the dock and Bilea politely waited his turn to disembark then exited on to the main street of Rueda Medina. Everything he needed was within a short walking distance.

He pushed on the heavy glass door and stepped inside the air-conditioned building. He made eye-contact with the employee seated behind a desk at the first cubicle. Lifting his laminated photo ID badge to shoulder height he introduced himself as Emanuel Bileaux, a variation of his real name. The employee was occupied with a client and merely nodded and pointed at the time-lock door near the tellers. Bilea waved an acknowledgement and strode confidently towards the back.

He flashed his ID at the closest teller, who activated the time-lock to open the heavy outer door. When he heard a click, he pushed the large handle down and entered the cubicle. The door automatically closed and locked behind him. He waited in the claustrophobic space until the interior lock buzzed, indicating he could enter the staff-only area. He pasted a friendly smile on his face and pushed the door open.

"Hola, buen día."

~

Dark watchful eyes followed the man with the satchel. He exuded confidence in every move, yet there was something sinister about him. Alexis Gomez couldn't decide if it was the dead expression in his eyes, or the taut awareness that he projected. He gave off the vibe of a wild animal willing to defend itself if cornered. Ostensibly he was a service technician working for the bank, but as a constable in the municipal policía Alexis' training was telling her otherwise. Her partner, and lover, Sergeant Felipe Ramirez called it her *Spidey-sense*.

Today she was dressed in navy shorts, a pink t-shirt and navy sandals. Her long dark hair flowed freely down her back. She was just another young woman waiting in the line. Like most locals she had learned to distrust the various ATMs and preferred the old school method; stand in line and get cash from the clerk.

Alexis tracked the man as he calmly identified himself to the staff, then assertively entered the time-locked vault. He seemed experienced, yet it appeared that this was his first time in this bank. Memorizing his features, she nibbled at the inside of her cheek. Short dark hair, thin face, trimmed beard, and fit build. Not Mexican or at least not Maya. Too lean and too tall.

"Alexis!"

She turned and smiled at the sound of her name spoken by a familiar voice. "Hola amiga." She said, leaning in to kiss her friend's cheek. A few minutes of back and forth chatter and then it was her turn to be served. She hugged and smooched her friend again, and handed her debit card to the teller.

"Dos mil, por favor." Alexis said to the clerk. Her eyes swept the secure enclosure, looking for the technician. He had moved further into the staff-only area and wasn't visible. She thumbed a message to herself, a reminder to describe him to Felipe.

The bank clerk pushed a piece of paper towards Alexis, asking her to sign the withdrawal. Then she slid the money and the debit card under the edge of the bullet-proof glass.

"Gracias," Alexis said tucking her phone in one pocket, and her cash in another. "Adios."

Outside Alexis slipped on her sunglasses and examined the street, looking for Felipe. She spotted the police cruiser parked in the shade near a large no-parking sign. She grinned to herself. He appeared to be enjoying air-conditioned comfort with his thick forearm pressed against the closed window. He might look relaxed, but she knew his observant eyes habitually scanned the street, sidewalks, and crowds. Cops survived to retirement by being watchful and wary.

She crossed the street and rapped a knuckle on the passenger's side window. He popped the door locks and shot her a sexy grin as she opened the door. "*Hola guapa*, you want a ride?" He bounced his eyebrows suggestively.

"Later lover. For now, could you swing past our place and I'll hop out?" She asked, settling herself in the passenger seat.

"Sure, anything for my princesa," He agreed, then asked. "Exactly how did we end up on opposite days off?"

"I owed a favour to Lucinda. She traded with me when my niece had her quinceaños last month."

"Claro, I'd forgotten. When do you flip back to your regular shift?" He said, putting the car in gear and checking for traffic over his left shoulder.

"Two more days." Alexis turned towards Felipe. "I saw a service tech in the bank that vibrated my antennae."

"Your Spidey antennae?"

"Si. He didn't look right."

"Why?"

"Too mean looking."

"That's it? Too mean looking?"

"Si, most of the techs are kind of nerdy. Soft. Sweaty." She popped one shoulder in a shrug. "Indoor guys."

Felipe turned his head and shot Alexis a questioning look, "Do you remember the Cancun State Policía detective, Cervera?"

"Sure, Marco reminds me of a grumpy old bear."

"More like a cranky grizzly bear," Felipe snorted. "Anyway, we chatted yesterday, catching up on what the bad guys are up to. Marco said several technicians have been recently killed in a territory squabble between the Cancun cartel boss Fuentes and a rival Romanian gang. The ATM company is panicking and hiring any warm body that can be trained to service the machines."

"Romanian. That's it. He's Romanian!" Alexis said excitedly bouncing her fist.

"Why do you think he's Romanian?"

"He's tall, slim, muscular. Short dark hair. Short dark beard. Dark eyes. Hawk-nosed. And that olive, Mediterranean skin tone."

"Or he could be Spanish, Israeli, or Italian. Just saying." Felipe said.

She waggled her hand, "Maybe yes, maybe no. But I'd bet on him being Romanian."

Felipe slowed the cruiser in front of their tiny casa. He let the engine idle and kept his foot on the brake. He turned to look at Alexis. "What are you thinking?"

"Inside job. He's messing with the card readers."

"I agree." He nodded. "Momentito. I'll park the car and call Cervera. You can give him a description of the guy." He pulled ahead one car length and shut off the engine.

"Let's go inside, it's more private," Alexis said. "Besides, I really need to pee."

Chapter 24

May 5th Cancun

"Adelante." Fuentes commanded. He recognized the light staccato rap of knuckles on his office door. Rodriguez.

"Hola. Buen día, Jefe."

"Buen día," Fuentes answered reflexively. Obligatory manners had become automatic by the time he was five, enforced by his tiny but ferocious grandmother. Long dead, he could still hear her stern voice. *Your father was a disappointment to me. He was nothing but a common criminal. You, will be a gentleman.* Sorry to disappoint you Abuela. I am also a criminal; although, I am reasonably well-mannered and very wealthy so, no, not a common criminal.

"I have interesting news, Jefe. Our informant with the Isla policía called me a few minutes ago," Rodriguez said. "A constable by the name of Alexis

Gomez has been checking through their pile of mug shots, looking for a man she saw in the bank."

"Why?" Fuentes barked the question at Rodriguez. Had she heard him, his *abuela* would have reprimanded him for his brusque tone. She never had to keep ambitious thugs under control, instead she had two willful grandsons who unwittingly sped up her imminent arrival at the cemetery. He had adored the woman who had single-handedly raised the orphaned toddlers. He still regretted every bit of heartache that he had caused her. *Go away, old woman. Leave me in peace.* For seemingly the ten-thousandth time he shoved the memory of her voice behind a door and turned the key, muffling her affectionate scolding.

"Gomez is sure the guy works for the ATM company and thinks he is fiddling the readers."

"Did she find his photo?"

"Si," Rodriguez nodded, "According to our informant, she is pretty sure she recognized him but doesn't know his name or where to find him." Rodriguez continued, "Based on his physical appearance tall, slim, short dark hair, short dark beard, thin face, dark eyes and olive-coloured skin she's convinced he's middle European, likely Romanian."

"Probably working for that Romanian, Adrian Bortos, we've been hearing about," Fuentes growled. "Why didn't the policía just ask the bank manager for a name?"

"According to our informant, Gomez and her partner Sergeant Ramirez are being very secretive. They don't know if any of the bank staff are in on the scam."

"Makes sense," Fuentes agreed. "Tell our snitch to send us a digital copy of that photo – immediately. As soon as you get it, forward it to all of our informants on the island and at the ferry terminal in Cancun." Fuentes said, as he leaned his elbows on his desk and tapped the tips of his fingers together. "If he's still on the island – I want him snatched when he returns to Cancun."

"Si, Jefe."

"We'll have a little chat about their operation and his boss Adrian Bortos," Fuentes said. Once he had finished interrogating the man, the crew would dispose of his remains somewhere in the jungle.

"Claro," Rodriguez concurred. He texted a quick note to their mole working for the municipal policía. "Anything else Jefe?"

"Have a van and crew on standby at the ferry terminal."

"Claro."

"Shut the door when you leave," Fuentes said, turning his attention to a stack of papers on his desk. He snorted in amusement. Even he, the king-pin of a cartel business, had legitimate bills to pay.

~

Putting on sunglasses to shield his eyes from the late afternoon sun, Bilea stepped off the Ultramar catamaran at the Cancun passenger ferry terminal. He smiled pleasantly at the pretty female who stood at the top of the ramp, thanking the passengers and wishing them a good day.

Behind the darkened lenses his eyes restlessly swept the dock, his neck prickled with tension. He couldn't locate the source of his unease. A number of the passengers exchanged friendly greetings with each other; some were returning to the island from Cancun, and others were headed from Isla to their homes in the city. They either worked for the same companies, or had become acquaintances while commuting back and forth. He had read somewhere that there were up to seven thousand workers commuting daily to and from the island.

Pretending that he was smiling at an acquaintance, Bilea searched the faces. No one in particular seemed interested in him, yet, he had a feeling of being watched. His gun was hidden under tools at the bottom of the satchel, too deep for him to reach quickly. *Rookie mistake, Bilea.* He mentally cursed.

His long-legged stride took him to the top of the ramp, past the sniffer dog and the government's latest attempt to slow the influx of recreational drugs to the island. An obviously brilliant bureaucrat had decided that the random red-light, green-light device similar to what recently been removed from Mexican airports should now be installed at the passenger ferry terminals in Cancun. The hot, lengthy line-ups produced passive grumbling over the absurdity of the situation. An innocent looking tour boat or fishing *panga*, could transport far more cocaine, marijuana, heroin, or fentanyl to the island than human mules.

As he passed the OXXO store at the top of the ramp he was momentarily distracted by the thought of buying a cold bottle of water, then two sets of strong hands clamped onto his arms and shoulders. "*Dracu*," He cursed loudly in Romanian, twisting and lashing out with a booted foot. One of his assailants grunted, but his grip didn't falter.

The two men quickly propelled Bilea towards a white van idling with the side door wide open. Bilea's face hit the floor. The two men leapt inside and smashed their knees into his back and legs.

Another man slammed the door and the van sped away. Behind his right ear, a gun muzzle dug sharply into his flesh.

"One move and you are dead, amigo."

Bilea remained still. There was no point in hoping that his kidnapping would be reported to the policía. It had happened too smoothly. Probably a minimum of four people; two abductors, a third to secure the van's door and a driver primed to stomp the gas and flee. People would instinctively know it was cartel-related and it wasn't healthy to get involved. He was on his own.

He had information. Whoever had ordered his abduction wanted that information. Maybe, just maybe he could trade for his survival.

Chapter 25

May 6th Isla Mujeres

Can we pull this off? Carlos leaned against a wooden gate, scrutinizing the small marina that they were negotiating to buy. It was a huge financial gamble that typically wouldn't be anything but a minor blip on his stress radar, but now he had Yasmin and hopefully, soon, a family to think about.

He ran a hand over his normally clean-shaven chin, and felt a slight stubble. *Huh.* With his Mayan ancestry facial hair was rare and shaving was an uncommon occurrence. He was surprized that Yasmin hadn't mentioned it this morning. He had woken up with a taut erection, the kind that frequently appeared first thing in the morning making it difficult for him to pee until it had subsided.

Laughing at his predicament Yasmin had said, "Let me help you with that." She had rolled on top of him and enthusiastically put his stiffy to good use. Once they were spent and satisfied, he had rushed to the baño before she could commandeer the toilet. Worse case scenario he could have urinated in the shower although his beautiful wife didn't approve of his bachelor habits. *I'm saving water*, he had guilelessly said the first time she had caught him. *That didn't go over very well.*

Carlos felt a wave of contentment sweep over him. The month of May was his favourite time of year; light winds, a calm ocean, very little rain, low humidity and mating season for many critters including turtles, iguanas, and birds. He smiled at that thought; mating.

Maybe we made a baby this morning. That would be amazing. A boy or a girl – it wouldn't matter, just as long as the child was happy and healthy.

"Hey Carlos!" A male voice shouted. "Are you taking a siesta?"

Carlos lifted his hand in acknowledgement, "Hey yourself, Pete. How're you doing?"

Wearing only paint-stained shorts the tall, sixty-something-American padded barefoot towards Carlos. He was thin and with long ropy muscles and his skin was baked to a leathery nut-brown. He looked dried up, desiccated from years of living on a sailboat in the tropics. His long white ponytail hung limply down his back, a memento from his younger days. He called himself Peter, Pete, or sometimes Pedro depending on his mood. The man was an enigma, never telling too much about his background but always friendly and smiling.

"I'm doing good for an old fart. "How're you?" Pete said as his calloused hand grasped Carlos'. Slab hard and dry, Carlos thought he was gripping the leather sole of a well-used work boot.

"Todo bien, gracias."

"I've been hearing rumors that you are buying this marina." Pete's unruly white eyebrows lifted inquiringly over his faded blue eyes.

"Really, where did you hear that?" Carlos temporized.

"Cut the crap, Carlos. It's all over the island," He retorted. "Are you going to kick out us long-term renters, like that other a-hole did?" He swung an arm backwards, indicating several boats tied up to the finger-floats.

Carlos knew the man was referring to a recent, and reportedly dishonest, marina take-over that had seen several live-aboard owners denied access to their boats and belongings. "Yasmin and I are thinking about buying the property, but we are a long way away from actually closing a deal," he replied, trying to be truthful but wary of divulging the details.

"But, if you buy it, are you kicking out the live-aboards?" Pete persisted.

"If ... we buy it," Carlos emphasised, "We might increase the moorage rates to help pay for improvements."

"Bullshit! You'll probably kick us out." Pete grumbled.

"Pete, I don't know if we are buying the property. We are thinking about it," Carlos replied. His eyes strayed to the motley collection of sailboats and cruisers secured to the dock. He knew a few had been abandoned by previous owners, unwilling to maintain the boats and unable to sell them to anyone else. The hulls that were slowly sinking at their berths would have to go. As for the owners who paid their monthly moorage fees, they were welcome to stay. Some of the boaters had become permanent residents while others were only temporary, staying just long enough to repair their boats and restock their provisions before pushing farther south to Belize.

He admired the independent, eccentric people who thrived on the adventures of long exploratory sailing trips. Carlos and his family were friends with many of the older generation of gringos who, when they were in their thirties and forties, discovered Isla while sailing the Caribbean Sea. Several families from the same area of the eastern seaboard in the USA had purchased large pieces of land along Sac Bajo in the 1970's. At the time there were no roads, no electricity, and no city water. The city of Cancun didn't officially exist until 1976. It was a quiet fishing village on a sandy beach. Supplies and building materials had to be brought from Merida or Valladolid.

The pioneers of the *gringo* residents told entertaining stories of making-do and learning to speak Spanish that were oddly similar to the stories that his parents told about when the foreigners settled on their island. The stories were mirror-images – dealing with a different culture, and a different language. The *gringos* joked about the locals and the locals joked about the *gringos*. Despite their differences many enduring family-like relationships had formed between the two communities.

Carlos sighed. Sadly, with the recent influx of more non-Spanish speaking property owners Carlos felt as if his Mexican culture was being crushed and devoured, like a boa constrictor eating its prey. More inhabitants meant more money for the business owners and their staff, but it also meant the erosion of the close-knit island life that he so loved.

"Hey, are you still in there?" Pete impatiently waved a hand in front of Carlos's face.

"*Lo siento*, Pete, I was reminiscing about the old times." His humour-filled gaze met the hard glare of the older man.

Pete's expression softened and he smiled wistfully. "Yeah, I miss those days too." He snorted a laugh, "I remember the first time I saw you and your younger brothers. The whole bunch of you were skinny-assed and barefoot, and digging up the sand on the corner of Rueda Medina and Matamoros. All I could think of was what the hell are those little devils up to?" Pete started wheezing and hacking. Between talking and laughing his cigarette-abused lungs struggled to snatch enough oxygen to keep him alive.

Carlos grinned. He waited until Pete regained his breath then said, "That's how we earned our pocket money."

"I know. I hung around to watch," Pete said, "and figured out what you were doing."

"It was pretty ingenious if you think about it," Carlos said. "We'd dig up the corner by the stop sign, then wait for a truck or car to arrive. The driver would stop and the wheels would sink into the soft sand."

Pete hacked another ragged cough; his eyes gleamed with laughter.

"As soon as the wheels started to spin Roberto, Nicolas and I would magically appear and offer to help the driver. We'd toss a few rocks in the holes, and then push on the back bumper until the vehicle was free."

"Not much traffic in those days."

"Claro, but enough to pay for our treats," Carlos replied.

"Weren't you worried the driver would catch on to your trick, and just drive off once you had *helped* him?"

Carlos held his hand palm up, and tapped it with his left index finger, "Payment in advance. Always."

Pete coughed a phlegmy laugh, "A true entrepreneur."

Chapter 26

May 6th Cancun

Fuentes turned the laminated tag over in his hands; Emanuel Bileaux also known as Emanoil Bilea. Likely both names were fake. Thanks to a sharp-eyed informant on Isla Mujeres, Bilea had been grabbed as he walked through the ferry terminal. The man had tried to trade his life for information on his boss Bortos, offering to work for Fuentes from inside the Romanian gang. Fuentes could never trust a weasel who turned on his previous boss to save his own life.

And from everything he now knew about Bortos, the man was too smart to fall for the fox-in-the-henhouse trick. After seeing Bilea's injuries Bortos would never have believed that his operative had escaped from Fuentes, or survived an interrogation without giving up valuable information.

Setting the identification tag aside, Fuentes picked up one of the Bluetooth readers Bilea had stashed in his work satchel. The Romanian crew had smuggled the gadgets into Mexico from China. They transmitted debit card numbers, pin codes, and names continuously. Bortos' employees only had to be within range of the transmitter to capture the information. Ingenious.

Once they were installed, the readers were almost impossible to detect. These tiny devices were throwing the money distribution system into disarray as fewer and fewer people trusted ATMs; any ATM. He wanted these money stealing gadgets for his enterprise.

But first things first. His second-in-command Rodriguez, and a group of enforcers were in the process of eliminating the Romanians. He'd given Rodriguez specific instructions to find the remaining supply of the Bluetooth devices and the data collector.

He'd lose a few of the young, inexperienced attackers in the raid but more were readily available. A recruiting trip to the poor hinterland villages and he could acquire as many as he needed with promises of unimaginable wealth and a guarantee to take care of their aging parents. The wannabes were cheap labour, and easily convinced. Many of the twenty-something men died violently before their thirtieth birthday, and their parents could be bought off for less than five thousand American dollars. That was pocket change in his world.

His biggest challenge was waiting. Waiting for Rodriguez to return and report. Until recently Fuentes had been the one leading the action, not sitting like an accountant behind a desk stacked with papers and files. He picked up his phone and unlocked the screen with his thumbprint. He started to call Rodriguez for an update, then reconsidered. Rodriguez was probably just a little bit busy, Fuentes thought. A wry grin twisted his lips. The man would call when it was over. If he was killed, one of the others would report to Fuentes in a move calculated to become his new lieutenant. It would be interesting to see which punk had the *cojones* to try for the job.

The phone still cradled in his hand Fuentes stared at the photo of Jessica Sanderson. Her smile; it was beyond description. The phone warbled disrupting his trance. He checked the screen. Rodriguez.

"Que pasa?" Fuentes barked into the phone.

"I'll be there in ten minutes," Rodriguez replied and disconnected.

Fuentes glared at his cell. *Something was seriously wrong. Rodriguez was never disrespectful.* He pulled his Glock out of the drawer, checked it and rested the gun on his desk. No damn way he was going to be shot down like a stray dog.

~

Rodriguez rapped on the closed door and then crossed himself. This could go either way.

"Adelante."

He turned the handle, pushed open the door, and stared at the ominous Glock aimed straight at his heart. He kept his hands away from his sides and open in a non-threatening gesture. "I apologize for being abrupt on the phone, Jefe. I was angry and frustrated." He watched Fuentes' eyes as the man slowly lowered his gun, resting it on the desk.

"You had me worried, Ventura." Fuentes didn't remove his hand from the gun. His finger still lightly touched the trigger. "Report," He commanded.

"The building was cleaned out, empty. Someone must have warned them we were coming." Rodriguez was exhausted. The adrenaline rush had dissipated, leaching his energy. He desperately needed to sit down but had to remain standing until the boss gave him permission.

"Did you search for the ATM devices?"

"Si, we searched everywhere. There was nothing but a few pieces of old office furniture, a handful of coffee containers and food wrappers." He flexed his toes inside his boots. It was something to concentrate on besides the beginning of a monster headache. "They hadn't been gone long. One cup of coffee was still warm."

Unlike his predecessor Fuentes didn't rant and rage at his lieutenant or blame him for the failure, instead he motioned Rodriguez to a chair. "Sit."

Rodriquez gratefully sat, keeping his hands visible on the arms of the chair. "Gracias, Don Alfonso." The glare of the overhead lights produced a pain that could only be described as someone shoving blunt needles into his eyeballs. Next would come the flashing lights, tunnel vision, and nausea so bad he would be on his knees puking into the toilet. *Mierda*, now was not the time to get a freaking migraine.

"Who, besides you and I, knew the address of our target?"

"Only Lopez and Osorio. I told them to dump the body, then meet us. It could be either of them." Rodriguez briefly closed his eyes willing the hammering in his head to stop. His eyes cracked opened. From the other side of the desk Fuentes silently stared at him.

"Are you ill, Ventura?"

"It's nothing. Just a headache, sir," He said, fighting down the urge to vomit.

"Then take your medications and get some rest. Report back here at nine, sharp." Fuentes flipped his left hand at his subordinate, dismissing him. "We'll deal with Lopez and Osorio then."

"I'm fine Jefe, let's deal with them now." Rodriguez knew he was losing credibility because of the damn headaches. In the past when he was just one of the many enforcers, he had been able to conceal his problem. Now that he was the number-two man, and dealt directly with Fuentes there was no way to hide his debilitating headaches.

"When you have a migraine, you are useless to me." Fuentes' face twitched with cold anger.

"Lo siento, *Don* Alfonso." Rodriguez stood and nodded politely. Even the slightest movement hurt like a son-of-a-bitch. *Right now, if he had to choose between the migraine or Fuentes shooting him in the head, he was tempted to choose the quicker death.*

Chapter 27

May 6th south of Playa del Carmen

"*Madre de Dios*," the man whispered in wonderment. A wild jaguar. Incredible. A muscular, gold and dark-spotted shape lifted its head to stare into the headlights of his transport truck. The animal's eyes reflected an eerie green.

Instinctively moving his foot from the gas to hover over the brake the driver prayed to the Mayan deities that this god-like beast wouldn't run onto the roadway. He wouldn't be able to stop the vehicle in time. The stunningly beautiful *Balaam* would be crushed under the twenty-four wheels of his heavy rig, reduced to a mess of torn flesh and bone splinters.

The animal remained stationary, protecting its feast. The driver expelled a long sigh of relief, crossed himself and continued his journey towards the capital city of Chetumal, located on the border of Mexico and Belize. The state of Quintana Roo was home to about half of the remaining four thousand wild jaguars, and he had just seen one.

What an experience! Surely this was a gift from God to see such a rare and divine creature.

When he got home, he would tell his youngsters about seeing the famous *Balaam*. His father had told him stories of growing up in a tiny jungle village and listening to the big predators roaring at their competitors; chasing other cats away from potential mates or protecting their food supply. The animals ranged in size up to a hundred and fifty kilos, or about three hundred pounds. The larger ones were typically male and prolific hunters. A jaguar's jaws were powerful enough to kill their prey by biting directly through a skull and into the brain. He shuddered. *What a horrible way to die.* And that brought back the image of the animal he had just seen. It had been feasting on something, and that *something* was covered by cloth, perhaps clothes. He swore forcefully, then placed an anonymous call to the State Police.

He kept his call short and powered off his phone. No damn way he was going to get involved in a policía investigation. It was common knowledge the first person to be suspected was the person who found the body.

Just keep on driving and keep your mouth shut. This never happened. The story would have to wait for another ten or twelve years, until his children had their own children. Then he could be the eccentric *abuelo* telling his *nietos* fairy-tales and fantastic adventure stories.

~

Detective Dante Toledo straightened up, "This is getting to be annoying." He groused to his partner Detective Marco Cervera as he wiped his new Giorgio Brutini slip-ons on a tuft of brittle grass. "Extremely annoying."

"Si, another unidentified corpse." Cervera's eyes skittered across the mutilated body and peered into the dark, foreboding tangle of trees and vines. Not all of the dead guy's extensive injuries were manmade. His right hand rested on the butt of his pistol, listening for the big cat. It had reluctantly, and noisily, forfeited its meal to the intruders. He could hear it growling and grumbling in the bushes. It was waiting until they left to resume its feast, or to drag the remains into the underbrush and bury it. *Las botanas*, a snack for later in the day.

"*Lo siento, gatito, I'm sorry kitty* – we're taking your supper with us," Cervera murmured.

"And why are we here on our own?" Toledo groused. "Where are the uniforms?"

"It's been a busy night in Playa with misbehaving drunks and automobile accidents. They're occupied."

Toledo fastidiously stepped around the body. "Why do we always get a messy murder scene when I am wearing good shoes?" He grumbled, indicating the chunks of raw meat laying in a puddle of body fluids and mud.

"Stop grumbling like an old woman," Cervera glanced at his partner's feet. "Just quit buying expensive shoes, then maybe the murder count will go down."

"And do what? Sit around all day and play Spider Solitaire on my computer?"

"Sure, why not? Cervera shrugged. "Do we know who called it in?" Their job would be simpler with a witness to question.

"Anonymous tip," Toledo replied. "According to dispatch it sounded like the guy was driving something big, like a truck, when he phoned."

"They get a trace on the call?" Cervera asked. He was relieved that Toledo had stopped whining about his damn shoes and had resumed his role as a proficient detective.

"No, too short and now the phone isn't communicating."

"Smart, doesn't want to be delayed," Cervera snorted.

"Or blamed," Added Toledo.

A roar of frustration exploded out of the gloom, lifting the small hairs on Cervera's forearms. Involuntarily he squinted at the dark jungle, searching for a feline shape. *Madre de Dios, the animal was angry.* "What's the ETA on the snipers?" He asked. The endangered jaguars were protected, but if it attacked, he wasn't going to just sit there and be the dessert course. Hell no, he would fire all twelve rounds at the carnivore if necessary.

"They should be here soon," Toledo said. "Did you see the monstrous size of those paw prints?"

"They're called pugmarks," Cervera replied, swiveling slowly in a circle. *Don't move quickly – a cat is a cat is a cat. A sudden movement will entice it to pounce. Where the hell was it? It had gone quiet, as if it was stalking them.*

"Pug-what?"

"The paw prints of big cats are called pugmarks."

"Whatever. They're huge."

"Si, exactly why I want an accurate ETA on the snipers," Cervera said, then held a finger to his lips. "Shhh. Listen." He heard a twig snap off to his left, the opposite side of where the cat had last let out a bellow of rage, and resentment.

"*Maldito!* It's hunting us, Toledo whispered.

"Cover my six," Cervera used the slang for standing back to back with guns drawn. His chunky rump collided with Toledo's skinnier butt. "Call dispatch."

"Claro," Toledo's gun dipped slightly as he swiped the screen.

"Tell them to haul ass. Lights, sirens, horns. Get here before we're cat food."

"More like cat shit," Toledo muttered, holding the phone to his ear.

Cervera grunted in agreement. The jaguar would eat first, then shit later. *Mierda, he had never been this afraid in his life. He was a city boy. Give him a drug lord, or a Russian gang any day of the week, not this silent and efficient predator.* Salty liquid leaked from his hairline, threatening to cloud his vision. He carefully swiped at the moisture with his left arm, then steadied his gun with both hands.

"Five minutes," Toledo said.

Only barely in contact with Toledo's back, Cervera felt his partner stuff his phone in a pocket and then regrip his gun with both hands. The faint wail of a siren could be heard coming from direction of Playa del Carmen.

"Let's hope they don't mean five Mexican-minutes," Cervera replied. He wasn't joking. In the Mexican culture time was fluid. It was only a suggestion of when the person might, or might not, arrive.

They *abso-fricking-lutely* needed these five minutes to be five minutes or less.

Chapter 28

May 7th Isla Mujeres

Parked in the shade with the air conditioning running and his cell phone on speaker, Ramirez and Alexis listened to Detective Toledo's tale of their encounter with a ferocious jaguar. For some reason the story made Ramirez think of the dubious ATM tech Alexis had noticed.

"Any photo ID on the body?" Ramirez asked.

"A Cancun driver's licence. We ran the name. It's fake," Toledo answered. "As far as we can tell the photo is right. His face looks like he was used as a punching bag but the cat seemed more interested in the body."

"Can you message me a copy?" Ramirez asked. Inside the sedan Alexis shot him a questioning look. He twitched one shoulder in a why-not? gesture.

"Why are you so interested?" Toledo asked, with a chuckle in his voice. "I just wanted to brag about the two city boys taking on a wild jaguar and surviving."

"Si, and it's a great story Dante," Ramirez agreed. His relationship with the Cancun detective had slowly morphed from professional, to casual acquaintance, to friendship. More importantly, he trusted him. "But something is niggling in my brain about this dude."

"Momentito."

Ramirez could hear Toledo fumbling with the keys on his phone, then a minute later his pinged with a message alert. "Got it." Ramirez opened the attachment and turned the screen so that Alexis could see it.

She took the phone and carefully studied the bloody image, then nodded. "Si, I'm sure that's him."

"Dante?" Ramirez said, checking to see if his counterpart was still listening.

"Si, I'm here."

"Alexis recognizes him."

"*Verdad*? What's his name?"

"Ah, well, that's a long story," Ramirez said as he prepared to tell the state cop the entire sequence of events. "A couple of days ago ...," He started to say.

"Not so fast," Toledo quickly interjected. "You offered to buy us dinner the next time we came to the island."

About to protest that he had never made that offer Ramirez heard a note of caution in the detective's voice. "Si, I did," He said, pretending he agreed with Toledo. "When are you coming to Isla?"

"Today. How often do the ferries run?"

"Every thirty minutes from Puerto Juarez. Call us when you are on the ferry. We'll pick you up at the main entrance."

"No worries. We'll meet you," Toledo responded.

"Remember I am a poorly paid municipal police sergeant so don't expect a gourmet meal."

"How about that place on the beach, the one that has great fish and chips."

That's weird. Toledo knows the name of the restaurant is Bally Hoo, but he seems reluctant to mention it, Ramirez thought. "Okay. Will we see you soon?" He queried.

"Si, soon."

"What was that all about?" Alexis asked, when he ended the call.

"I'm not sure. Toledo suddenly became evasive." Ramirez tucked his phone away, and put the car in drive. "Apparently I'm buying the four of us a meal at Bally Hoo."

"Great, I feel like a good steak."

"Tacos. Our budget is limited to steak tacos."

"Cheapskate."

"I live with a woman who keeps close tabs on me. She suspects I have a girlfriend." He tossed her a cheeky smile.

Alexis turned her head and aimed her eyes at the window.

~

"Why so secretive, Dante?" Ramirez said, after the initial pleasantries and greetings were dispensed with. "We're on duty. Turning off our phones is against regulations." The four policía huddled around a table situated away from the bar staff, but not in the prime location favoured by tourists.

Toledo and Cervera exchanged a wordless glance, a silent communication sent and received.

Cervera rested his forearms on the table, "We are uncertain about our privacy. My daughter showed me how our phones can be tapped through a bunch of free apps." Cervera dropped his voice a little more, "So, you give us your info. We give you our info. We all turn our phones back on and have a nice gossipy chat about jaguars or deep-sea fishing, or whatever comes to mind. Agreed?"

Ramirez looked at Alexis. She curtly agreed. "Claro." Aiming for an ostensibly relaxed demeanour Alexis thought they looked exactly like what they were; four paranoid cops who didn't know who was a friend and who was an enemy.

"May I get you a drink?" The waiter asked appearing tableside.

"Si, and we'll order our food at the same time," Alexis said, doing a quick visual confirmation with the others. She felt as if she was an extra in a B-grade, spy-thriller; cast in a scene that was so poorly scripted it would be deleted during editing. She wanted to make this meeting as short as possible because all sorts of shit could happen while they were out of communication. And if the Comandante found out? She didn't want to even think about that.

Once the waiter had taken their orders and moved away, Cervera motioned to Alexis. "You first, Constable Gomez."

She nodded, then succinctly recounted the series of events that led her to believe the ATM technician was bogus, starting with her watching the guy in the bank. Convinced he was part of the Romanian gang operating out of Cancun she scrutinized the stacks of mug shots until she found a matching photo. Unidentified, but for sure a bad-guy. "Did I forget anything, Sergeant?" She asked Ramirez.

"Not that I can think of," He answered, then discretely motioned towards the two waiters who were approaching with their drinks and food.

"Do you need anything else?" Asked the original server.

"No, gracias. I think we have everything," Responded Cervera.

Waiting a minute or two while the waiters moved out of hearing range, Cervera began itemizing what they knew about Bortos, the rumoured head of the Romanian gang infringing on territory controlled by Fuentes the current king-pin of the Cancun cartel.

Cervera gave Ramirez a knowing look, then leaned close to his ear and whispered. "Does she know?"

Even though the older man's lips were as still as a ventriloquist's when he whispered the question, Alexis knew he was asking her partner if she knew their secret. Toledo, Ramirez, the Federal officer Antonio Martinez, and Cervera had anonymously helped Fuentes survive an execution.

"Remember my lunch with these clowns a few months ago." Ramirez said, his eyes searched her face.

"Si, it's all good," Alexis confirmed. No one really knew why, but the previous cartel boss had suddenly begun a campaign of executing small-time competitors and his activities had caused widespread panic in the tourism industry. The American news channels like Fox, NBC, and ABC used sensationalized reports to increase their market share. Their newscasts were overrun with dramatic headlines: *Mexico is dangerous. Don't go there.* Droves of frightened tourists had cancelled their winter vacation plans.

"Bueno," Cervera said, "unfortunately our new friend is also being naughty."

Toledo said, "He was good until the new neighbours moved in. Now, the numbers are on the way up."

Alexis understood exactly what they were alluding to; the Romanians were infringing on the cartel's territory and the body count was climbing. The muscles in the back of her neck burned with tension. She rotated her head, flexing the tendons and let her eyes drift across the restaurant. An overhead television showed live images from Texas. "*Mierda*, those poor people," She said, "another mass shooting in the US."

Ramirez turned and watched the headlines scrolling across the bottom of the screen.

"I just don't get it," Alexis said, her eyes glued to the muted television. "When our bad guys kill each other, Mexico is violent and dangerous. When twenty innocent people were mown down in a shopping centre with a semi-automatic weapon the media hounds wring their hands and wail, but within days they'll lose interest and move on to a different tragedy. It never changes."

"No, it doesn't," Toledo agreed.

"And there is frick all we can do about it," Cervera muttered. "Okay, are we done?" Cervera reached for his phone, "If we are, let's check for messages then chat for fifteen minutes before Dante and I leave."

"If you don't trust our cell phones how do you plan to keep in touch?" Ramirez asked.

"My wife, Beatriz, is a fabulous cook," Cervera said, "you are all invited to our house for dinner in a week. Okay?" He held his phone at table height so the others could see what he was doing, and pushed the power button. "That jaguar really was amazing. Such a beautiful, and terrifying animal," He said, winking at the others.

Paranoia runs deep – as the song said. A paranoid cop might live to be an old cop. Maybe.

Chapter 29

May 8th Isla Mujeres

Carlos poured the strong coffee into two tall mugs, then added the hot foamy milk and attempted to draw a heart with a drizzle of caramel syrup. It was a bit lopsided, but Yasmin would get the idea. Her *frilly coffee*, just the way she liked it.

At the beginning of their relationship he had tried to switch her to his preference; hot, strong, black, and unsweetened. Instead she had converted him. It wasn't worth the struggle of making two different types of beverages every morning, and coffee in bed was her one special treat. Every single day. He chuckled, okay, there usually was that *other* special treat that they both enjoyed. Morning sex.

"Mmm, gracias, mi amor," Yasmin said setting her cup on the night table, then lifting her face for a smooch.

"My pleasure," He said, and walked around to his side of the bed, then set his coffee down while he stacked his pillows against the headboard. Satisfied, he settled his butt in the bed and leaned into the pillows. "By the way, when I was in Cancun yesterday buying supplies for the *Loco Lobo,* I bought you a little gift."

"Lindt dark chocolate with caramel and sea salt?" She asked.

"Oh, I'm sorry," His shoulders sagged and his smile turned down, in a caricature of a sad clown. "I didn't know you liked dark chocolate."

A grin playing across her lips she held out her left hand, motioning, *give it here* with her fingers.

He reached inside the nightstand and slowly extracted a large chocolate bar, the exact brand and flavour that she had mentioned. "Is this what you like?" He dangled it just out of her reach.

"Diablo! Give it to me," Yasmin dove across his lap and snatched the chocolate from his hand.

Carlos quickly looped his arm around her body, pulling her close and kissing her thoroughly. "You took the bait. I caught me a pretty mermaid." Coffee and chocolate were forgotten as desire swept through his body. He lost himself in her beautiful green eyes.

"Will you marry me, beautiful lady?" He asked again, as he had done every single day since he had originally proposed to her. He had made himself a promise that if she said yes, he would never take her love for granted. He would propose again, and again, and again, until their time on earth was finished. And then he would continue proposing when they met in the next world.

"Si, mi amor. With pleasure."

Carlos kissed her deeply one more time, then gently pushed her upright. "Seriously, I did buy you a gift. But you have to get dressed to see it."

About to take a drink of her coffee, Yasmin stopped and studied him. He could almost see the thoughts whirling in her head, wondering what he had bought.

"May I finish my coffee first?" She asked.

He shrugged nonchalantly, "Sure, if you want." He swung his long legs out of the bed and stood, "I'm going to shower. Take your time." Carlos ambled to the bathroom. Smiling to himself he looked at his one indulgence; a heavy Rolex watch that he never removed from his wrist, not even when sleeping or showering. *Three minutes. Three minutes tops.*

"Why do I have to be dressed to see my present?" Yasmin raised her voice so that he would hear her.

Carlos checked his Rolex. *Ninety seconds. That was fast.* "It's not at our house."

"Where is it?" Yasmin asked, padding naked into the bathroom. She flipped up the toilet lid and sat down.

While she peed, he kissed her again. "Get dressed and I'll show you."

She flushed, rinsed her hands and hopped in the shower. He moved in behind her and as soon as the water was a comfortable temperature started soaping her body. "If you keep doing that, I'll never see my gift." She moaned leaning into his hands.

~

Forty minutes later, showered, dressed, and caffeine coursing through their veins, Carlos held up his hands in mock surrender. "Stop badgering me woman. I'll show you your present as soon as it is ready."

A text pinged on his phone. Yasmin watched his face as he read the message. Whatever the text was, it had made him smile.

"*Perfecto*. Come with me Princesa," He mocked bowed, one hand resting on the door handle. Yasmin straightened a make-believe tiara and gathered an imaginary princess gown with both hands, then daintily flounced past him.

"What ...?" She stopped to stare open-mouthed at a double-cab, dark orange truck parked at the curb with an enormous red bow stuck on its hood. "... is that?" She pointed at the large vehicle.

"A Toyota Tacoma. Isn't she a beauty?" Carlos answered, his eyes gleaming with happiness as he handed her a key fob. "This is yours; I have my own."

Her first thought was to laugh hysterically, or at the very least snort derisively, but she snuck a look at his face. He had a ridiculously happy grin aimed at the hulking monster. She just couldn't utter the superficial agreement that a more traditional wife might have said; *yes dear, it's lovely, it's exactly what I wanted*, so she carefully picked her words. "Well, it's big. And bright. Everyone will certainly see us coming."

What she wanted to say was, *what the hell were you thinking? It's huge, and wide, and ugly with a monstrous thing mounted on the front that looks like it could shove a full-grown bull off the road. It will be a nightmare to drive on our narrow streets that were built before cars had been invented.*

"Exactly. It'll be much safer than my low to the ground Porsche. Come on, let me show you."

Biting the inside of her mouth to keep from laughing out loud, Yasmin followed Carlos. He opened the driver's door, and motioned her to get in. The sill of the four-door truck hit her at about mid-thigh. She considered her short skirt. *Madre de Dios, I hope no one posts this on Instagram.* She hitched up one slender leg and hopped on the other foot, boosting her slim body on to the seat.

"I thought you didn't like SUVs. Didn't you say they were too big for our little island?"

"True, but it has lots of room for our niños, and maybe a dog," Carlos was still in his enthusiastic salesman mode.

"You do realize we don't have kids?" She asked. "Or a dog?"

"Si, but we are diligently trying to make babies," He said, suggestively bouncing his dark eyebrows, "and we can adopt a dog from either one of the rescue societies on the island."

"You big goof, you think you have all the answers," Yasmin huffed a laugh. "Do you remember a long romantic dinner at Limón when a very handsome man earnestly promised me — *we'll buy a sensible family vehicle of your choice, carina.* Do you remember that conversation?" She asked.

Carlos threw back his head and belly-laughed, "Si, I do remember. But I fell in love with this beauty." He stuck his head inside the cab and kissed Yasmin, "Lo, siento, mi amor. I couldn't help myself. She bewitched me."

"But why orange?"

"Simple. Pedro has a white truck, and Diego has a black Jeep. I wanted a different colour." He winked, "And I happen to know that you look stunningly gorgeous when you wear that orange Spandex dress."

Orange. Because he likes my dress. And men thought women had peculiar logic.

Chapter 30

May 8th Cancun

His wearisome two-week break from his equally tiresome job of installing underground pipes in Minneapolis was over. It was time to head back home.

What a freaking waste of time and money.

He had returned to the island hoping to rekindle his enjoyable and sexy relationship with Jessica Sanderson, instead she had treated him like a smear of dog shit on her shoes.

He had been polite, apologetic, and considerate. He'd sent her a conciliatory note asking her to meet with him. He had offered to buy her dinner, lunch or even just pay for her coffee and a stupid muffin but she had flatly refused. Then her two pet gorillas, Diego and Pedro, warned him to stay away from her - or else. He'd nearly crapped his pants when they had cornered him at the café.

Outside the passenger ferry terminal in Cancun, Whitecross tossed his carryon bag into the filthy white and green taxi. He had bypassed the cleaner, more expensive cabs parked under the shade of the parkade and flagged down a beat-up junker at the curb. A roving driver typically charged less because they didn't have to pay a percentage of their fares to their *sitio,* their home-base.

"Amigo," The driver shouted. "Are you getting in or not?" He pointed impatiently at the empty back seat.

Whitecross yanked his focus from the past and into the present. He eyeballed the driver and shook his head, "No, I've changed my mind." He reached inside, grabbed his bag and banged the door shut. The driver cursed at Whitecross for wasting his time and for slamming the door on his precious piece of crap.

"Yeah, same to you buddy," Whitecross said, hoisting his middle finger as he strode back across the road. Inside the terminal he pushed open the glass door to the air-conditioned souvenir store-cum-ticket sales office and paid for a return trip to Isla Mujeres.

Time to man up. He wasn't going to leave with his tail tucked under his ball-less butt. He'd tell his boss that his flight was delayed. He was rapidly running out of cash, but still had a virgin credit card that he could hit to cover his expenses.

One more day should be enough time to sort her out.

~

Fuentes cracked the throttle open on his powerful Yamaha Road Star 1700, blasting past passenger cars and the huge *doble remolque* trucks as he roared along the four-lane toll road, the Mexican Federal Highway 180D. He was speeding towards the colonial city of Valladolid for only one reason. Stress release.

After all the years that he had sought to be the top dog, the jefe, the cartel king-pin he now realized it wasn't the dream job he envisioned. He was surrounded by incompetent, scheming rivals who wanted to wear the crown, but the only way to do that was to eliminate the reigning monarch – him.

Oh, poor you. In his head he could hear his grandmother chiding him for feeling sorry for himself. The old woman wouldn't be proud of what he had become, but she also wouldn't allow him to wallow in self-pity. She would have said, if you are going to do a job, any job, do it properly.

The raid on Bortos' location had gone badly; someone had tipped them off and the place was cleaned out. He wasn't any closer to eliminating the Romanian intruders and every day that passed he was losing more credibility among his crew. He was in danger of being assassinated by the young punks who thought they could do a better job. Even Rodriguez was a concern. His lieutenant supposedly suffered from debilitating migraines, but perhaps it was a cover story to excuse his unexplained absences and recent failure. He could be working with the Romanians, not against them.

Fuentes forcefully twisted the throttle increasing his speed, yet again. The tarmac rushed under his front wheel at an exhilarating rate. All it would take to send him tumbling into oblivion would be one unmarked pothole, or a patch of loose gravel slopped from a poorly maintained dump truck. The spectre of death straddled the passenger's seat, its cold breath tickling the back of his neck.

If he was going to die, this was the way to go.

His blood fizzed with adrenaline!

Fuentes arrived back at his compound feeling energized and extremely horny. He strode into his living quarters and stripped down, then scrubbed off the sweat in a pounding hot shower. Strutting nude from the bathroom into his bedroom he picked up his cell phone and called Rodriguez.

"Send me that new blonde," He said, not bothering to identify himself. Rodriguez would know who was calling. "And a bottle of Veuve Clicquot champagne," He ended the call without waiting for a response.

Looking down at his hard erection he chuckled, "Mind your manners and I will let you play with our guest." He pulled on a pair of silk boxer shorts and sprawled on his sofa.

Hearing a timid knock at his door Fuentes commanded, "Adelante, come in."

The door opened and the slim young woman entered carrying two flutes and a bottle of champagne in a bucket of ice. Before she could open her mouth to introduce herself, he said, "*Silencio*. I don't want to hear your voice. And I don't want to know your name."

Her face registered offended surprise, but she obeyed.

She strongly resembled Jessica Sanderson. Slim, with long blonde hair hanging down her back and bright blue eyes, but she was Russian. He had heard her voice when they brought her to the compound and she didn't sound anything like Jessica. He didn't want her to ruin his fantasy.

Two hours later Fuentes pointed at his bedroom door, "Get out," He hissed.

The woman scrambled to find the silky robe she had been wearing and stumbled to the door.

He was angry and frustrated. No matter what the blonde had tried he hadn't been satisfied. He was on the verge of pummelling her but she just wasn't worth the energy. Better to leave her undamaged and useful.

Like an addict that needed a hit, Fuentes picked up his phone and stared at the photo. His hand gave him the release he craved. It was only temporary, then he would need another fix.

Chapter 31

May 9th Isla Mujeres

Jessica stopped her vehicle directly in front of the bank. It wasn't a proper parking spot but if she was quick, she could grab some cash from tellers and be gone before the municipal *policía* objected. It was just after nine o'clock in the morning and for the majority of the locals it was too early to be at work. The streets were empty. It was the peaceful lull before the mid-day influx of day-trippers from the Cancun hotel zone.

"I'll just be a few minutes, pooch. You stay and look after the *carrito*," She said to Sparky. She glanced at his leash, confirming he was tied to the steering wheel column. She strode towards the bank. "No line! Excellent."

Ten minutes later as she started to push the glass door outward a hand reached from behind her. "*Permíteme*," A man said, as he held the door open. She glanced over her shoulder about to say thank you, when something stirring in his dark eyes silenced her.

Sparky barked frantically pulling on this leash. Startled, Jessica glanced towards him.

Before she could open her mouth to hush Sparky, the man said, "Stay calm Señorita Sanderson."

"Who are you?" She angrily demanded stepping towards the street.

Clamping a hand over her forearm he pulled her close and said, "An admirer. Do. Not. Yell."

Her skin crawled with loathing. "You! You're the one who broke into my house."

"Be quiet and keep walking or I will kill you and your mutt." He motioned with his head for her to look down at his right hand. "I have a gun in my pocket."

Jessica could see a bulge in the side of his light jacket. It looked like a gun. She opened her mouth to scream for help, and he poked the barrel into her ribs.

"*Silencio,*" He forcefully whispered.

Blinking back tears of rage, she closed her mouth and stared at him. Her brain scrabbled for rescue options. She had to do something to save herself and Sparky. She couldn't let him get away with this. She wouldn't.

"We are going to get into your golf cart, and you will drive us to your home." He pointed with his chin to the vehicle. "If you don't shut that dog up, I will shoot you, then snap it's neck."

"You won't get away with this!" Jessica sputtered.

"I'm an experienced executioner," He jammed the gun harder into her ribs, causing her to suck in a painfilled breath. "I will be gone before anyone figures out what happened."

Hearing the self-confidence in his statement Jessica realized, for the moment, she had to cooperate. "Shush, Sparky, *tranquilo*. It's okay baby. Please be quiet." Jessica grabbed her dog by the collar as he lunged at her kidnapper. She cinched her other hand around his muzzle to muffle his barking.

"Use the leash. Wrap it around his snout!"

She started to protest, but the man's cold stare changed her mind. She struggled to untie the leash using just one hand, and reluctantly muzzled her dog.

"Get in, and keep him under your legs."

Jessica complied and clamped her struggling, angry dog between her left leg and the seat of the cart. Her eyes brimmed with tears of rage and frustration.

"I am an excellent shot with both hands," The man said, sitting close beside her. He shifted the gun to his left pocket. "Now turn around at the next corner and drive to your house."

Jessica did as she was instructed passing the passenger ferry terminal, then the car ferry docks heading south. She kept her head pointing forward but her eyes frantically searched for someone she knew. The traffic was still light but starting to build towards the usual snarl of vehicles on the narrow roads. Passengers in taxis were preoccupied with their phones their faces pointed down into laps. A few moto drivers passed by, but didn't notice her stress-filled face. Her hands were sweaty with fear, leaving wet spots on the steering wheel.

There. A black Jeep headed towards her. Diego. He beeped the horn twice and briefly lifted the fingers of his left hand. His classic, nonchalant greeting.

Jessica didn't respond. She stared straight head, then casually placed the open palm of her right hand on her left shoulder and tapped twice. She hoped the *pendejo* beside her didn't recognise the signal. She dried her wet palm on her shorts and regripped the steering wheel.

Please mi hermano, understand. She silently implored Diego.

~

Diego's concentration flipped between watching Jessica's tiny red *carrito de golf* disappear in his rear-view mirror, and the traffic in front of him. He drove north for another two streets, then he grunted a soft curse and swung the Jeep around. Something wasn't right. She wasn't smiling and Sparky was tucked under her legs on the driver's side, not enjoying his usual spot on the passenger's side. More importantly, she didn't look happy about the stranger sitting close beside her.

Without pulling over, Diego thumbed his phone contacts and put it on speaker.

"Bueno," Pedro answered.

"Hey Bro. I need your help." Diego's eyes continually scanned the streets looking for hazards; oblivious pedestrians, wandering dogs, or pigeons pecking at spilled snacks. He checked his side and rear-view mirrors, then the road ahead.

"Que pasa?"

"Jessica, Sparky, and some guy just drove by in her golf cart headed south along Rueda Medina," He said, "I beeped and waved. She ignored me."

"Was it Whitecross? Maybe they had a reconciliation and were busy chatting."

"No, it wasn't Whitecross," Diego replied, 'I didn't recognize him, and then she did that thing that Maricruz showed us."

"What thing?"

"That right hand touching the left shoulder thing."

"The military signal for danger?" Pedro asked.

"Si."

"Huh. Have you got her in sight?"

"No, I had to turn around. I hope she's headed home," Diego said, then yelled "Ah shit!" and the phone tumbled onto the floor.

"Diego! Diego!" Pedro's voice hollered at him from under the dash. "What's happening?"

Diego pulled to the curb, and reached for his phone, "A driver pulled out in front of me by the whale shark statue. He didn't even look. I nearly ploughed into a cart full of people."

"*Mierda*, are you okay?"

"Si, but I'm losing time." Diego checked his mirrors, and over his left shoulder and pulled into the assortment of taxis, motos, and other vehicles.

"Okay. I'll meet you at her place."

"Park a block away. We need to figure out what's going on."

"Claro," Pedro agreed, then added. "Should I call Carlos?"

"Si, and I'm going see if Ramirez is working."

"The policía sergeant? That Ramirez?"

"I have a very bad feeling about this."

"Okay, I'll be there in fifteen."

Chapter 32

May 9th Isla Mujeres

Driving one-handed, Diego scrolled through his contacts and found the private cell number for his acquaintance Felipe Ramirez. He turned on the speaker function and set the phone in his coffee cup holder.

Again, the call was answered with just a single word, "Bueno."

"Hey, Ramirez, it's Diego Avalos. Are you working today?" He half-shouted. His noise inside his Jeep was loud; the big engine and big tires were rapidly chewing up the distance.

"Si, Alexis and I just started our shift," Ramirez said, referring to his partner. "We are on until tomorrow morning." The municipal policía worked twenty-four hours on, and then twenty-four hours off. "Por que? Why?" He asked.

"I have a situation," Diego said, running through the sequence of events. He also described the recent break-in at Jessica's house. Ramirez had made no comment about it being an unreported event. Both men knew there weren't enough policing resources to do anything except make a note of the incident for a potential insurance claim. But since the only things taken were a few pieces of her lingerie, there wouldn't be a claim for reimbursement.

"Okay. We'll respond," Ramirez said, then asked. "Hey numb-nuts, are you driving and talking on your cell phone?"

"It's on speaker," Diego temporized. "Can you meet us at the cross street south of Jessica's house?"

"Why there?"

"Whoever is with her can't see anything from her casa because there is a taller house blocking the line of sight."

"Claro."

~

"Shit," Whitecross said, "She thinks I'm not good enough for her, but she lets that creep into her house." He stood with his mouth hanging open staring at the scene across the street from him.

Jessica Sanderson had just parked her golf cart. Some short-haired no-neck was obviously in a hurry to have some fun. He possessively gripped her arm and hurried her inside. Her mutt seemed to be struggling to get out of her grip.

Hmph. Guess I'm not the only guy that dog doesn't like.

He had intended to confront her last night but once he got to the island, he'd lost his nerve. He wasn't normally an argumentative person so he decided to have a drink or two first. *For Dutch courage* as his granddad liked to say. One drink had been quickly followed by a second. A third one had seemed like a really good idea. After that he had lost count. He woke facedown and drooling on a hard bed in a one-star hotel. Feeling nauseous he had gingerly showered, dressed and headed out for a substantial breakfast before catching a taxi to her neighbourhood.

Even though he had recently slid his note of apology under her door, it had taken him a few minutes to relocate Jessica's house. Using his limited Spanish, he told the driver the street name and described the building but similarity between the one he thought was hers, and her actual casa, was confusing. Apparently, bright orange walls with pink window frames and a shiny turquoise door was a popular combination in her neighbourhood.

The taxi driver had dropped him a few blocks away from his intended destination. He eventually got his directions sorted out and found her place just in time to see Jessica and her new boyfriend arrive.

To hell with that stuck-up bitch. Whitecross turned and stomped away. As he headed two blocks north to a busier road to flag another taxi a bright orange Toyota Tacoma passed by, momentarily distracting him from his pity-party. *Nice wheels.*

~

"You know, Jessica is going to be seriously pissed off if we barge in and she and lover-boy are in the middle of the best sex ever!" Carlos said as he joined the group assembled on the corner.

Diego nodded grimly, "I know, but I am sure she's in trouble."

"What a surprise," Ramirez said, with a snort. "Jessica is in trouble."

"Felipe, don't be a jerk." Alexis chided.

Ramirez gave her a look. "Really? How many incidents have we been called to in the last three years that have included Jessica and Sparky, or Jessica and Yasmin?" Ramirez retorted. "Sorry Carlos, no offence man."

"None taken, Ramirez. I agree, Yasmin, Jessica and Sparky have been involved in a number of misadventures," Carlos replied. "It's a lethal trio." He admired Jessica for her strength and sense of adventure but a small part of him hoped that she would stay out of trouble, or at least not drag the love of his life, Yasmin, into her future escapades.

"How do you want to handle this, Ramirez?" Asked Pedro.

"Me? You called us for help," He retorted.

"Claro, but you and Alexis are policía ... so, we will defer to your superior knowledge," Pedro countered. The right side of his mouth quirked up in a smirk. "And you have a gun."

Ramirez huffed out a breath of air. "You want me to be the fall guy when it all turns to shit."

"Verdad," Diego agreed.

"I'll knock on her door," Alexis offered, "and pretend I was invited for a cup of coffee."

"You're in uniform." Diego pointed out.

"I am wearing a t-shirt under my uniform," Alexis said as she quickly unbuttoned her dark long-sleeved shirt and tossed it into the cruiser. "Did you get a good look, Pedro?" She asked as he eyed her tight white singlet, clinging to her trim form.

His face pinked, "Si, but you are a lot easier on the eyes than your partner."

"The ladies like to check out Felipe too," She retorted, "Maricruz gave him the eye a few times before you were in the picture."

Ramirez groaned, "It was a little harmless flirting, Alexis. Can we just concentrate on Jessica?"

"*Por supuesto*, of course, but don't think I didn't notice." She spun around and strode towards Jessica's casa. As she walked, she repositioned her Taser to the small of her back where it was easily accessible but out of sight.

"Busted," Carlos said quietly, to Ramirez.

"Si, she's is very jealous and hot-tempered."

"And carries a Taser," Carlos pointed out. "I wouldn't sample other delicacies if I were you."

Ramirez shrugged nonchalantly, "Uncertainty keeps things fresh and exciting." He pointed at the Toyota Tacoma parked several car lengths back, "That yours?"

"Nice deflection, Ramirez, but yes, that's my new ride," Carlos answered.

"Sweet. What does Yasmin think of it?"

Carlos smiled, "She thinks I'm *muy loco*, but she still loves me."

Chapter 33

May 9th Isla Mujeres

Alexis instinctively stood to one side, out of the direct line of fire in case an armed assailant was lurking inside. Even though the bullet-proof Kevlar vests were hot, cumbersome, and not issued to every person on the policía municipal, right about now she would give her left boob to be wearing one.

Resting her right hand lightly on her Taser, she took a deep breath and rapidly sketched the sign of the cross with her free hand. Then she raised her fist and rapped her knuckles on the shiny turquoise door.

"Jessica. Hola, are you home amiga?" Alexis called out.

"Who is it?" Asked Jessica.

"Alexis. You asked me to come over for coffee this morning." She replied, "Did you forget?" Alexis pressed her ear to the door. She could hear two muffled voices quarreling inside the house.

Jessica's voice sounded stressed and brittle. The other one was definitely male, quiet but firm.

"Yes, I forgot. I'm sorry, Alexis. I'm tied up at the moment."

Alexis winced when she heard a thump like a fist hitting flesh; likely retaliation for hinting she was *tied up* instead of just saying she was busy. "Darn it, Jess, I walked all the way over here from my place," Alexis griped. "Can I at least use your baño and get a drink of water before walking home?"

"No!" Jessica replied. Alexis heard a sharp intake of breath. When she continued speaking her voice radiated pain. "Alexis, I'm sorry. I have the flu. I don't want you to catch it."

"Claro, okay, I understand," Alexis said peevishly. She hoped that she sounded convincing to the guy. "Call me when you are feeling better."

"Yes, I will. Thank you," Jessica said.

"Hasta luego, see you later," Alexis said then strode in the opposite direction. At the corner she turned left, and ran back to where the guys were waiting. She knew her breasts were bouncing with each stride, but to hell with it, she'd give them something to enjoy. Reaching the group, she bent over double for a moment to catch her breath. "She's in trouble," She said, then recounted the entire exchange plus the muffled sounds from inside the house.

"Do you think there is more than one guy?" Asked Carlos.

"I don't know, I only heard Jess and one male."

"Any idea if Sparky is inside?" Pedro asked.

Alexis shook her head, "I didn't hear any dog noises."

"Maybe the guy killed him," Diego interjected.

"Probably," Agreed Ramirez.

"Ideas?" Asked Pedro.

Ramirez huffed, "We call this in and get more help."

"There's no time," Alexis countered. "We have to help her now."

"Alexis, that's not protocol," Ramirez contradicted firmly.

"I know that, but the guy is really hurting her. I heard her gasps of pain, and there is no time to wait for a damn hostage negotiator to come from Cancun."

Carlos studied Alexis, "So what do you suggest?"

"I'm going back. I'm going to plead with her to let me use her baño, because I can't make it all the way home. While I am making noise and begging, Pedro, Diego and Carlos can sneak in through her back yard. Felipe and I will take the front door."

"Sounds risky to me," Pedro said. "He might kill Jessica."

"I don't think so," Argued Alexis. "She's his insurance policy."

Carlos looked at Diego and Pedro. "Alexis could be right. We may not have much time.

"I really don't like this," Diego said.

Pedro shook his head. "Me either."

"Ramirez?" Asked Carlos.

Ramirez glowered at the group, "The situation sucks and it's definitely against our rules, but Alexis is right. We have to act now."

"Fine," Diego reluctantly agreed. His eyes begged; *save her*.

Carlos pulled out his cell phone, "Alexis, call my number. I'll leave the line open so we can coordinate our attack on the back door." He recited the ten digits as she quickly thumbed her keyboard. His phone tinkled with a humorous tune that Yasmin had downloaded. Carlos touched the answer ikon, and slipped the phone in his breast pocket.

"Give us five minutes to get around the back." Pedro said.

"Let's hope this doesn't turn to shit and we end up getting her killed," Diego said, "I wouldn't be able to forgive myself if that happens."

"Si," Carlos unhappily agreed.

Alexis nodded, "Okay five minutes and we go." She tensely watched the three men run towards the corner and disappear. A few minutes later she heard Carlos say, *we're good to go*. She mouthed, *te amo, I love you*, at her partner and began to move towards Jessica's house. Hopefully, none of the neighbours would notice or report the strange happenings in the *barrio*.

Once again, Alexis banged her left fist on Jessica's door. Her right hand held her Taser close to her thigh. "Amiga, please. I desperately need to use your baño. I have diarrhea," She hollered. "I really can't make it home."

Without warning the door jerked open and a hard-looking man with a pistol in one hand reached for her left arm with his other hand, and jerked her forcefully towards himself.

Ramirez fired his Glock at the man's chest.

Alexis discharged her Taser into his crotch.

Then they simultaneously yelled, "Policía!"

The man's face contorted in pain and surprise as he slumped in an untidy heap. His feet were inside the house, and his head thumped noisily against the concrete entrance, like a pumpkin dropped on the ground.

~

Ramirez heard a splintering crash reverberate from the back of Jessica's house; the sound of someone kicking a wooden door.

"Jess!" Yelled Diego, "Jess, where are you?"

"Here." Ramirez heard her respond with a rasp in her voice. *Good, at least she was alive. He didn't hear any dog sounds. Sparky was probably dead.*

With his Glock trained on the man's chest Ramirez leaned over and felt for a carotid pulse. The stuttering beat faded away under his fingertips. He shook his head at Alexis. "Gone."

"Bueno," She said. "It would be a waste of resources to save his sorry ass."

Ramirez nodded indifferently at her caustic comment. He pulled out his phone, snapped a photo then thumbed a message to Detective Dante Toledo and hit send. Pocketing his phone, he said to Alexis. "Guess who this is?"

"You recognize him?" She asked, studying the dead guy's face.

"Si. Allow me to introduce you to Alfonso Fuentes, the head of the Cancun cartel." Ramirez gestured towards the body with a mocking sweep of his arm.

"What the hell was he doing here on Isla? With Jessica?"

"That's exactly what I intend to find out." Ramirez holstered his gun, and motioned Alexis inside. She lifted her booted feet one at a time over the corpse, taking care not to step in the blood pooling around his neck and shoulders. They followed the sounds of voices inside the house.

"Are you going to inform él Capitan?"

"In a few minutes. I want to chat with Señorita Sanderson first," He replied. He blanked his expression, keeping his concerns to himself.

Chapter 34

May 9th Isla Mujeres

"No, Diego, I don't want an ambulance," Jessica snapped. She pulled the blanket tighter across her shoulders to stop her shivering. *Just nerves.* Her face ached from his punches. Her neck felt as if she had whiplash. Her ribs throbbed, but she could inhale okay. It had all happened so quickly, as if he was in a frenzy. Fortunately for her, Alexis had interrupted his frenzy - twice, saving her from further abuse or perhaps death.

She wanted a hot shower, and clean clothes. She wanted to throw away this bra and thong that he had forced her to put on, and never wear turquoise-coloured anything ever again. She wanted to down two large whiskies and forget the entire nightmare. She wanted to scream, to cry, to destroy anything that asshole had touched, but mostly she wanted to cuddle her pooch.

"Where's Sparky?" Jessica yelled. Her eyes desperately searched for her dog.

"Easy, Jess," Diego answered. "He's in your guest room, wrapped with a shit-load of duct tape. Pedro is trying to free him. The little guy is frantic to see you."

"I want to see him, now," She started to stand, and felt light-headed. She grabbed at the bedside table for support and plopped her butt on the edge of the mattress.

"Stay there, I'll get him." Diego said, motioning at Carlos to keep her sitting down.

"I am not made of glass." She barked.

"Shut up, and sit." Carlos said, resting one hand on her slim shoulder. "Please, Jessica."

"You're a bunch of control freaks." Jessica muttered, watching Ramirez and Alexis walk towards her bedroom. *Just freaking great. More people to witness her utter humiliation.* The two cops stopped a few feet back from the bed. Ramirez crossed his arms and studied her face. She dropped her eyes, feeling wary of his shuttered expression.

"We just don't want you falling and cracking your head open. We have enough blood and stuff to clean up," Carlos wryly retorted.

"How bad do I look?" She asked.

Carlos didn't answer instead he held up his phone. "Yasmin's on the way. I sent her a message." His reassuring smile seemed forced, not genuine.

Diego arrived toting Sparky in his arms. The little guy trembled, vibrating the bits of tape still stuck to his fur.

"Oh, my poor baby. Give him to me," Jessica held out her arms but Diego placed the dog on the bed beside her.

"We need to look after your injuries first, Jess, before you try to comfort Sparky," He said.

"How bad do I look?" She repeated, her gaze squarely on Alexis Gomez. "Tell me, or I will crawl to the bathroom and check the mirror."

"Your left side is badly bruised. How do your ribs feel?" Alexis asked.

"They hurt like shit, but I can breathe so probably not broken," Jessica said, taking in a cautious and shallow breath to confirm her self-diagnosis.

Carlos headed towards her kitchen, "Do you have a bag of frozen peas? Or ice in your freezer?"

"Peas," She answered. The soft bag of cold peas would slow the bruising, and feel gentler than ice cubes when pressed against her aching body. "What else Alexis?"

"You won't be winning any beauty contests for a few weeks," Alexis replied. "Two black eyes, a badly bruised cheek. A bloody nose, but I don't think it is broken. It still looks straight," Alexis stopped talking.

"I don't understand why he beat you so badly and so rapidly," Diego said. "We came as quickly as we could," He added, his face was steeped with guilt and anger.

"Not your fault, *mi hermano*. I tried to get away as he was shoving me inside the house. I kneed him in the nuts and tried to run. When he grabbed me, I bit his hand," Jessica answered. "He got pissed off and started beating me." Jessica's look turned to smouldering hatred.

"How did he manage to wrap Sparky with all that tape, and still control you?" Ramirez asked point-blank.

"The son-of-a-bitch made me do it! He held the pistol to Sparky's head and made me wrap the tape around and around and around." Remembering the look of betrayal in Sparky's eyes she clearly stated, "I. Will. Kill. That. Bastard." She glared at the sergeant, defying him to contradict her.

"He's dead," Ramirez said, holding her angry glare. "I shot him."

"Oh," Her rage slowly leaked from her face. "Thank you," She whispered.

Ramirez didn't respond, instead he scrutinized the group, "Before I call this in, you heard Alexis and I yell *policía* before I fired. Claro?"

"Loud and clear," Agreed Diego.

"Si," Carlos said.

"Exactamente," Pedro confirmed.

A few minutes later Ramirez stuffed his phone in his pocket. "The shit is about to hit the fan. The Capitan is on his way, along with the coroner, and the doctora for Jessica." He held up his hand stalling her protests, "it's necessary for us to get an official report on your injuries. I know you want to get cleaned up, but please, don't do anything."

Jessica nodded wearily, "Si, I understand." She gently pulled Sparky closer to her thigh. "I need to see for myself that the asshole is dead." She reached out a hand. "Diego, help me." It wasn't a request.

Diego gently slipped an arm around her battered body. "Why don't I just carry you Jess?"

"No! I can do this," She retorted, pulling herself to her feet. Sparky jumped off the bed, dogging her heels as she slowly shuffled to the front door.

Diego and Jessica stopped a few feet away from the corpse, avoiding the blood.

Sparky marched straight through the congealing liquid, then lifted his leg and urinated on the dead man's face.

"Sparky no!" Jessica rasped. Her dog momentarily looked abashed, then continued to empty his bladder on the guy who had treated his best friend so badly. "Sparky!"

"The coroner is going to love that," Carlos said, "But the poor little guy is humiliated. He couldn't help you this time."

"Even superheroes don't win every battle against the forces of evil," Diego said, with a sad smile.

~

"Jessica!" Yasmin yelled from the street. She slammed the taxi door, and ran towards the house. "Jess."

"Yasmin, wait!" Carlos leapt over the corpse to intercept her.

"Mendoza! What the hell are you doing?" Sergeant Ramirez shouted at Carlos. "Don't you dare come back inside until I tell you to!" He roared.

"You can't go in." Carlos wrapped his arms around her, blocking her view of the corpse, "It's a crime scene."

"I'll go in the back way," She retorted, pulling against his grip.

Carlos shook his head, "There's a new house under construction. You have to scramble through the worksite and then climb over the fence." He said pointing at her short skirt and sandals. "Just wait a bit, carina."

"Jessica needs me."

"Yes, she does. But you have to wait until Sergeant Ramirez says you can come inside."

"You jumped over the dead guy. I can jump over him too."

"No, you can't," Carlos shook his head, "Ramirez is furious at me for that. We have to stay out here until he gives us the okay."

"*Mierda*! Arrogant bastard. Who does he think he is?" She asked, angrily pointing at the house.

"Ramirez is a good guy. He came when we asked him for help," Carlos replied, "and he's probably in deep shit with his Comandante."

"Why would a police officer be in trouble for responding to a call for help?"

"He killed the guy, then he told his *capitan* that Alexis Gomez and he had responded to a call for assistance."

Yasmin's eyebrows lifted in understanding. Bureaucratic crap had a way of oozing to the bottom of a tank, suffocating the lowest person in the muck. Both Alexis and Ramirez would be worried about the noxious currents flowing towards them.

"Okay, then," She said, "I'll wait until for permission to enter the house." She dialled Jessica's cell number, and listened as her friend whispered a hello. "How are you holding up, Jess?"

Chapter 35

May 9th Cancun

"Madre de Dios!" Toledo swore.

"Que pasó?" Cervera asked. His gaze pinged to his partner's face then bounced back to the chaotic Cancun traffic. Cars zigged and zagged from lane to lane, jockeying for openings wherever they appeared. His driving philosophy was simple. If the front will fit, the back will follow.

"What are you looking at?" Cervera queried his silent partner. Toledo was staring at the screen on his phone.

"Pull in here," Toledo said, pointing his chin towards the parking lot for Home Depot.

Giving his partner a puzzled look, Cervera swung the aging plain-Jane sedan into the lot and parked in a rare and prized shady slot. "What's going on?"

Toledo handed his phone to Cervera, "This came in a few minutes ago. It's from Ramirez on

Isla Mujeres. I was busy with another message and just opened it now."

"Huh," Cervera said staring at the photo of a very dead Alfonso Fuentes. "What the hell was he doing on Isla?"

"No clue," Toledo replied. "But more importantly, who's the next lowlife in line for the throne?"

Cervera thought for a minute, "Either his lieutenant Ventura Rodriquez Sosa, or his younger brother Matías Fuentes."

"Matías? I thought he was married with kids and out of the business."

"Nah, he's still involved," Cervera said. "Remember the old saying, you don't divorce the cartel, the cartel divorces you."

"So, dirt-bags will be killing other dirt-bags. Again."

"Si, it will be a war zone while the opponents battle to be the top dog."

"But, with God's help," Toledo sketched the sign of the cross on his chest and kissed his right thumb, "maybe this time there will be fewer survivors."

"I didn't know you were a believer, Dante, but if you have a connection with *Him* that would be helpful," Cervera said, and returned Toledo's phone. "Call Ramirez and find out what happened."

Isla Mujeres

Ramirez felt his phone vibrate in his pocket. He checked the screen, then ignored the call. He would phone Toledo later when he had more information.

He returned to the corpse and bent down, riffling through Fuentes' pockets. He couldn't figure out what the drug lord was doing on the island, by himself, and kidnapping a gringa. Something just didn't add up. He used two fingers to tweak a phone out of a side pocket and slid his fingers across the screen. It was password protected, but the background screen gave him his first clue; a photo of a stunningly beautiful Jessica Sanderson in a dazzling blue dress, smiling happily at someone off camera.

Moving back inside the house, Ramirez said, "Jessica, do you recognize this photo?" He turned the screen so that she could see the image.

"Holy shit!" She grabbed at the phone, but Ramirez quickly lifted it out of her reach.

"Please, don't touch it."

"That's me, at Carlos and Yasmin's wedding in February."

"Are you sure you don't know this guy?" Disbelief crept into Ramirez' voice.

"No, I don't know him," She protested.

"Why does he have your photo on his phone?"

"I don't know," Jessica met the man's suspicious stare. "He might be the waiter who rubbed up against me when I was helping Yasmin to the ladies' room. The same guy that disappeared after the shooting. Remember? Someone wounded my Auntie Pattie at the wedding and then shot at me the next day outside the Ultramar terminal."

"Yes, I remember," Ramirez agreed.

Jessica glanced at her barely-clothed body, wrapped under a large blanket. "He's definitely the same guy that broke into my house recently. "This," she plucked in disgust at the bra strap, "is my missing underwear which I will incinerate as soon as you are finished interrogating me."

"Señorita Sanderson," Ramirez reverted to cold formality, "this man was the head of the powerful Cancun cartel. Are you telling me that this is just some sexual fantasy he was indulging in?"

"I. Don't. Know!" She yelled startling everyone, including Sparky. "I don't know him. I don't know why he has my photo on his phone. And I sure as hell didn't know he was a cartel drug lord!"

Diego flipped a smouldering look at Ramirez, "The questions can wait until Jessica is cleaned up and rested. She's been through a lot."

"The Capitan will ask tougher questions," Ramirez snapped, then turned his hard eyes on Diego. "If you have involved Alexis and me in the cartel's business, I won't forget or forgive."

Diego's head snapped back as if he had been punched in the face, but Jessica answered before he could open his mouth to protest the accusation.

"Sergeant Ramirez, I am not, nor would I ever be a girlfriend, lover, informant or associate of any person involved in the cartel. I swear. I don't know what's going on," Jessica stated. Too angry to cry her blood pressure pounded in her veins. She rubbed her left temple as a spike of pain shot through the side of her head. *How dare he assume she was some little plaything of a cartel boss?*

Ramirez grunted and turned away.

Outside on the street were the sounds of too-late sirens and slamming doors; the doctora, the coroner, the capitan and also their comandante. The word had spread. A notable criminal had been killed ensuring the comandante's gold-braid and glittery shoulder-boards would appear in the news reports and photographs.

~

"Señorita Sanderson." Camara all but clicked his heels together as he smirked at her.

Oh hell, not him again! Jessica pulled the blanket closer, wishing the odious little man and his piggy-eyed stare would instantly relocate to an alternate universe. The Comandante Julian Camara disliked her intensely, accusing her of causing trouble on his otherwise peaceful island in paradise.

"Comandante," Jessica tipped her head in pretend politeness, while envisioning him stuffing his fat face at the wedding dessert buffet. After the shooting it had been chaotic at the beach club; officers rushed to secure the perimeter, the doctora and Red Cross assisted her Auntie Pattie, panicked guests pleaded to leave with their children while Comandante Camara fastidiously selected a stack of delicious goodies.

"We meet again, and so soon after your last debacle, in, what was it? February? Yes, I believe it was only February the 22nd since I last had the pleasure of your company." He all but licked his porcine lips when he surveyed her attire.

"It is always a pleasure to see you, Comandante," Jessica replied. Even on a good day her ability to be superficially pleasant was extremely limited. She preferred sincere conversation to playing nice, but she refused to smile or to look away. She wasn't going to let him embarrass her with his obvious delight that she was battered, bruised and almost naked. *Do your best, I am tougher than you think.*

Chapter 36

May 9th Isla Mujeres

Yasmin's long legs were curled under her, much like when she was a teenager, and reading a good book.

What she was reading wasn't a book, and it wasn't entertaining. It was awful. Horrible. Disgusting.

Facebook, Twitter, Instagram and Snapchat were clogged with photos of the outside of Jessica's house; some were snapped from across the street, others were taken with the aid of a drone. The pictures revealed the tangle of police cars, the coroner's van, an ambulance, and television news crews. The images were captioned with wild guesses, innuendo and gossip about Jessica and the cartel boss.

Someone had lurked on her Facebook page and downloaded images of Jessica, then posted them along with photos of Fuentes' corpse. The posts accused her of being his mistress. His lover.

His personal assistant. His informant. Or the supplier for the small-time pushers that populated the restaurants and souvenir stores in Centro.

People that had never spoken to her were condemning her because she was a victim; a terrified human being who fought to escape and was badly beaten for resisting.

Comments and counter-comments ran through every social media page that Jessica had joined.

If you hang around with criminals you get what you deserve.

She shouldn't live in Mexico, it's dangerous.

What was she thinking, allowing him in her home?

It serves her right for being involved with drugs, and drug dealers.

How could people be so cruel? To condemn a person they had never met, never watched her face light up with love when she was with her family, or close friends. Never seen her competently handle her Auntie Pattie's life-threatening wounds, and couldn't hear her now as she sobbed quietly in her bedroom.

And as for being involved with drugs! That was an outright lie, malicious slander. Jessica didn't use drugs, sell drugs, buy drugs, or let anyone use drugs in her home. What people did in their private lives she didn't care about, and didn't try to control.

People could be so hateful.

Yasmin unfolded her legs, and tip-toed to Jessica's bedroom door. She listened and could hear Jessica whispering to Sparky, trying to reassure herself and him that they would be okay.

"Jess?" Yasmin quietly asked, "May I come in?"

"Si, Yassy," Jessica sniffed loudly. "But can you grab the roll of paper towel in the kitchen, first? I've used up everything else."

"Of course, and how about a cold drink?" Yasmin cracked the door and peered inside the gloomy bedroom.

"Sure, just water please. The doctora gave me pain killers. She told me not to mix them with alcohol."

"Or, maybe you should have a cold beer and then try to sleep," Yasmin said. *Anything to keep her from scrolling through the hateful comments on the internet.*

"No, not yet. I have to let Sparky do his business in the back yard," Jessica said, sliding her feet to the floor. "I'll join you in the kitchen. I need to stop feeling sorry for myself."

"No, no, Jess, please stay in bed. I'll open the back door for Sparky."

Jessica held up her phone. "It's okay, Yassy. I know what's on the internet." Her lips held a sad, hurt smile for a few seconds then gave up the fight. Her tears spilled over and ran down her face.

"Oh, Jess." Yasmin stepped forward and awkwardly tried to hug her friend without touching her battered body. "People can be such *pinche pendejos!*" She said, wishing she could eliminate the cyber filth.

~

Jessica sniffed loudly and disengaged from her friend's embrace, "I really do need paper towel for this snotty mess." She said, limping towards the kitchen. Sparky clung to her heels, afraid to let her out of his sight.

She stopped at the back door, and opened it. "Come on Sparky, you haven't had a pee for hours." As soon as she spoke the shocking image of him pissing on Fuentes corpse came to mind, and she started to giggle. She gingerly held her ribs, breathing deeply. She could hear exhaustion, stress, and a touch of hysteria in her laughter.

Yasmin skimmed a puzzled look at Jessica, "What's so funny?"

"You weren't here when it happened. Sparky peed on the dead guy's face." She wiped her eyes, and hiccoughed twice.

Yasmin's hand briefly covered her mouth, then she snorted a loud unladylike laugh. "Why did he do that?"

"Carlos said Sparky was getting his revenge, because he couldn't help me."

"The poor little guy," Yasmin said. "He must have been desperate to help you."

"The coroner wasn't very happy about it but once she saw my injuries, she understood the reason." Jessica took a breath and held it, counting slowly to ten then released the air. That seemed to help, so she did it again. Her hiccoughs and giggles subsided. Jessica wrapped her right arm around her friend's waist, and leaned on her. "Thank you so much for being here. I love you, my friend."

"Igualmente," Yasmin replied giving Jessica a very light squeeze as they shuffled into the living area. "Where do you want to sit? Kitchen or living room?"

"The kitchen. The hard chair will be better support," Jessica said, sitting down. "I've changed my mind. I would like a beer. Maybe it will help shut my brain off for a few hours."

"I'll get it," Yasmin reached in the refrigerator and pulled out a bottle of Playa Norte, made by their friends at Isla Brewing. She cracked open the bottle and poured the amber liquid into a glass. "Here you go," She said, setting it on the table. "I'll join you."

Settled at the table with their drinks, Yasmin took Jessica's free hand in hers and said, "What can I do to help?"

"Get a pair of scissors and remove the rest of the freaking tape that is stuck on Sparky's fur," Jessica said, as she bleakly looked at her pooch. Pedro had tried his best to remove the adhesive binding, but the dog had struggled and fought. He was determined to be with Jessica. Pedro had only managed to cut the duct tape from around his muzzle, and his legs. His fur still carried chunks of the ominous grey tape.

"Oh, my God, I didn't even notice," Yasmin leapt up and headed to the cutlery drawers.

"I tried to pull it off, but it hurts him too much," Jessica said.

"Where do you keep your scissors?"

"Far right, second drawer."

"Got them," Yasmin said. "Now what?"

"Sit on the floor and call him. He'll sit between your legs," Jessica said, "Then just cut the tape off. I don't care if he's bald when you're done, just get that damn stuff off my dog." Her vision blurred; like trying to see through a rain-splashed window. She took a long slug of cold beer, and hoped it would shut off the non-stop images running through her brain.

"Are you going to call your family?" Yasmin asked as she snipped at the tape and dog fur.

"Mañana. Or maybe mañana, mañana," Jessica said, meaning, *it's probably not going to happen, ever*. She dreaded the conversation, letting her close-knit family know that she was once again involved in a police investigation. She smiled uncertainly at her friend, then popped one shoulder up in an anxious shrug. "It's Mexico. Why do today what you can put off until tomorrow."

Chapter 37

May 10th Isla Mujeres

"No, Mom, I'm sorry. I can't come home right now," Jessica said. She picked up her coffee, carefully. Movement of any kind was painful, but larger movements like reaching for her coffee cup were excruciating. As long as she stayed still and didn't do anything stupid, like sneeze or laugh, she could survive the pain.

The left side of her torso resembled an abstract painting; a canvas of colour smeared with varying shades of purple, black, red, orange, and a touch of yellow around the edges. Her muscles were stiff and contracted; the body's natural response in attempt to protect her ribs.

Jessica sipped a bit of the hot liquid. *Brain food! Essential, to keep her functioning.* She hadn't slept more than twenty or thirty minutes. The combination of pain medication and the one beer hadn't been able to dull the incessant pain or stop the vivid nightmares.

And she had only told her parents an abridged version of her encounter with Fuentes, leaving out the part about the two ugly shiners, her battered nose, and bruised ribs.

"Why can't you come home?" Anne Sanderson asked. "We'd love to spoil you while you rest."

Closing her eyes her mom's face appeared on her eyelids. Anne Sanderson's face held a few more laugh lines in the corners of her eyes but she and her only daughter were very similar in appearance, with bright blue eyes, smooth skin, and thick blonde hair. Jessica desperately missed her family.

It was right around sunrise in Vancouver, Canada, when Jessica had called, but she knew her parents would be up; either getting ready to go to work, or just enjoying a cup of coffee on their expansive back deck. Her mom was an emergency room nurse. Her dad and two large brothers, Jake and Matt, were firefighters. They were all shift-workers, but her parents had enough seniority they could pick the shifts that suited them. Like Jessica, they were early risers.

A light step alerted Jessica that Yasmin was awake too. She put a finger to her lips, warning Yasmin not to speak and then pointed at the pot of coffee. Yasmin silently nodded and quietly fixed a cup of coffee for herself.

"Mom, do you mind if I put you on speaker? It's easier than holding the phone to my ear." It really would be easier to set the phone on the table, but she had been trying to keep her voice down on the assumption that Yasmin was still asleep.

"Go ahead, I have you on speaker so your dad can listen in." Anne said, "Honey, are you sure your FaceTime app isn't working? I would feel better seeing you."

"No, it's not functioning Mom. I'll try and reload it later today," Jessica motioned *zip-it* to Yasmin, then activated the speaker function. There would absolutely be no FaceTime calls until the bruising had faded.

"I can't leave for a bunch of reasons." Jessica said, "The biggest one is the comandante thinks I am guilty of something, of what he hasn't yet decided, but he knows I'm guilty."

"What! That's ridiculous." She heard her dad, Gord Sanderson, yell in the background.

"It is what it is, Dad," She said, "I'm just lucky he hasn't arrested me."

"Bloody hell, that's outrageous!" He raged. Tall, ginger-haired, and in great physical shape for a middle-aged man, Gord Sanderson, was typically calm and easy going. But when it came to his not-quite thirty, and only daughter he could be as protective as a mama grizzly bear.

"Anyway, I also can't take Sparky on the plane this time of year. The heat embargo for pets traveling in cargo is in effect, and he doesn't fit under the seat. He's too big." Jessica looked down at her stocky dog. He was too long and definitely not flexible enough to fit into a soft-sided carrier that had to be stuffed into a small space designed for two human feet. *Nope. He wouldn't fit.*

"Then why don't I take a week off and come visit you?" Anne suggested.

Jessica gestured to Yasmin, pointing at her battered face and mouthed. *Hell no!* "Honestly, Mom, I'm fine. My friends are spoiling me and Sparky is right by my side."

"Alright, but I would feel so much better seeing you," Anne finally conceded, "Please try to get your FaceTime app working. Or maybe you can borrow Yasmin's phone and call us back?" She suggested.

Jessica quickly motioned to Yasmin; *don't answer*.

She tipped her head in silent acknowledgement and smiled knowingly at Jessica.

"Sure, I'll ask her when she gets up," Jessica said, as she studied Yasmin's amused expression. "She doesn't typically get up until ten-thirty or eleven."

Yasmin compressed her lips together, stifling her retort.

"Okay, honey. Please call us every day. We are very worried about you," Anne said.

"Yep, pumpkin, we love you," Gord added. Jessica could hear the emotion in his voice. Damn, she hated putting them through more stress.

"I love you both so much. Give my love to Jake and Matt." Jessica said. "Love you, chat later." She ended the call, and looked at her friend.

Yasmin pushed her phone across the table. "Why don't you use my phone and call them back?" She said, her words taunting Jessica.

"You know I can't do that. If they saw this mess," She pointed at her bruised face, "my dad would be on the next plane. He would want to avenge his baby girl's honour."

"If you don't look after yourself ... I have their phone number." Yasmin stated.

"That's blackmail."

"Si, it is, and what are you going to do about it?"

Jessica stuck her lower lip out and coolly regarded Yasmin, "Before you got up, I was thinking about how I really missed our pizza and wine nights, our special *seesta*-time." Jessica said, purposely mangling her pronunciation of sister. "We haven't seen much of each other since you've become an old married woman," She stared across the table at her friend.

"And?" Yasmin said motioning for her to continue her thought.

"Now, I realize I don't miss you at all. You're just a manipulative brat."

"Ooooh, you shouldn't call me bad names, or I'll call your mommy." Yasmin waggled the phone back and forth.

Jessica snorted one laugh then wrapped her right arm around her torso, cradling her ribs. "Please Yassy, don't make me laugh. It hurts too freaking much." She took a few shallow breaths, then removed her arm. "Seriously, I really have missed our *seesta*-time."

"Si, me too," Yasmin agreed. "Between work, spending time with Carlos, and the day to day stuff, there's no time to spend with my bestie."

"Uh-huh. Time with Carlos," Jessica said, making air quotes with the fingers of her right hand. There was no way in hell she was going to lift her left arm up any further than her belly button. "Translates to sex, lots of sex."

"True. But did you ever hear that old saying about the first year of marriage?" Yasmin asked, "The one about putting a peso in a jar every time you do the *chucka-chucka*?"

"Yep, but in Canada it was a penny not a peso. Then, after the first year you take out a penny every time you do the happy dance, but you'll never empty the jar," Jessica said, "Same joke, different currency."

"Well, we are trying to fill our jar," Yasmin said, "Plus make a baby."

"Wow, I am so happy for you," Jessica said, gently reaching for Yasmin's hand, and gave it a light squeeze. "I had no idea you wanted to start a family."

"We do and we're really excited about it," Yasmin said, then added, "Did you see Carlos' new toy?"

"You mean that big orange thing? What the hell was he thinking buying a monster truck?" Jessica looked at the expression on Yasmin's face. Her lips were quivering as she tried to hold back her laughter. Jessica grinned, and clutched her ribs. Between the stiff neck, the spikes of pain in her torso, and her facial muscles that screamed with every facial expression she didn't want to laugh. But, despite the searing pain it was hard to keep the chuckles contained.

"According to Carlos it is perfect for our children and a dog." Yasmin dead-panned, "And the colour matches one of my dresses that he is likes me to wear."

"It matches your dress?" Jessica said, "that's the funniest thing I've heard in a long time."

"I know."

"Wanting kids, I understand, but a dog?" Jessica snorted. "You're not exactly a dog person."

"I love Sparky," Yasmin retorted.

"Now, you do. But when we found him you thought I was bat-shit crazy to take him home with me, on your new moto." Jessica said. Her lips tweaked up at the memory of the heated disagreement they had had over Sparky. Yasmin was adamant that she didn't want him anywhere near her. Then Jessica had added fuel to the argument when she asked Yasmin to stop at a corner store to buy dog food. She had reasoned that she needed to hold onto the frightened animal, but he needed food, so therefore Yasmin had to be the one to buy it. Yasmin had petulantly complied.

"That was then, this is now." Yasmin said, reaching under the table and carefully patted

Sparky's head. "Poor boy, he's had a very rough year."

"Yes, we all have had a difficult year," Jessica said gripping Yasmin's hand. "And, I really do miss our goofy conversations."

"Si, me too, *seesta*. Me too."

Chapter 38

May 10th Isla Mujeres

"Come. On. Felipe," Diego said, as he repeatedly shoved his fingers though his short dark hair. Pacing back and forth, he eyed the ankle-twisting assortment of his children's toys strewn across the floor of their tiny living room. "You don't seriously believe that Jessica was involved with Fuentes?"

He had asked Ramirez to come to the house for a private talk, just the two of them. Cristina had readily agreed to take their baby daughter for a visit with her mom and dad. His in-laws were just a block away and they doted on sweet little Ana. Their three niños, their boys, were in school for another hour. Diego was hoping the privacy would encourage Ramirez to truthfully answer his concerns.

"I am having a hard time swallowing Jessica's story." With his butt parked squarely on the wooden chair Ramirez had a mulish look on his face. His muscled forearms were crossed over his broad chest, and he radiated a vibe of controlled anger. "One of our techie whizz-kid patrolmen figured out the password. There are more photos of her on his phone, a lot more."

"Are there any of them doing the happy dance? A little chucka-chucka perhaps?" Diego facetiously asked. He was probing to see if any of the photos proved that Jessica was sexually or romantically involved with Fuentes.

Diego believed with all of his heart the answer was no, but Ramirez seemed to be operating on the premise that she was guilty until proven otherwise. It wasn't that big a surprise to him because until very recently the entire legal system in Mexico operated on the Napoleonic belief of guilty until proven innocent.

The French had governed Mexico in the 1860's just long enough to install their atypical system, making life in Mexico even more convoluted. *Thank you, France for the little gift that keeps on giving.*

In 2008 the Mexican government changed to an adversarial judicial system similar to the United States, but it wasn't fully implemented until 2016 leaving the courts in a tangled mess for eight years. Many Mexicans did not know about the changes, either through apathy with the government or because they never had the occasion need a lawyer's assistance.

Ramirez twitched his head about a millimetre in a negative motion, "No, just pictures of her."

"Exactly!" Diego's right index finger shot into the air, emphasizing his point. "He was stalking her."

"Or he didn't want his face floating in cyberspace."

"*Madre de Dios*, Ramirez, you know her. We all know her. She's a good person."

"*I had no idea. I thought he was a good person*," Ramirez cocked an eyebrow, "That's a direct quote from a recent newscast. The neighbours thought the guy was decent, until he shot twenty people in Texas."

"Honestly man, I can't understand why you think Jessica was involved with Fuentes." Diego dropped his body into a kitchen chair, causing the wood to groan with the sudden weight. The chairs were at least twelve years old, and tiny tropical insects had been feasting on the wood. One day he was going to land on his ass in a pile of kindling. He shoved the thought aside, "He hurt her, he hurt her dog, and before that he broke into her home."

"Maybe she likes it rough, and he just got carried away," Ramirez flatly stated. "It wouldn't be the first time that we've responded to a domestic dispute that started out as rowdy, consensual sex."

"No, not in this case." Diego abruptly stopped his pacing. "She signalled me that she was in danger," He intuitively mimicked Jessica's gesture crossing his right arm over his chest and tapping his left shoulder. "She was not a willing participant."

"She's good friends with her neighbours Enrique and Rosa. Why didn't she scream for help?" Ramirez probed.

"He had a gun stuck in her ribs," Diego angrily retorted.

Ramirez said, his detached expression hadn't changed since he parked his ass in the chair. "I'm not the only one doubting her actions, or her character," He stated.

"*Mierda!* Most of the crap that gets posted on social media is innuendo, gossip, and fake-news mixed in with pictures of cute kittens and puppies."

"True," He agreed, "but a lot of her friends are asking interesting questions."

"No. Not her friends." Diego said, vehemently shaking his head. "Her friends, Yasmin, Carlos, Pedro, Maricruz, Luis, Cristina and I believe in her, as do our families. We all know she's a good person. The doubters can go straight to hell."

"Well, I'm out of it for the moment," Ramirez said. "The Comandante has suspended Alexis and I, pending the outcome of his personal investigation."

"Ah, shit, man. I'm sorry. I had no idea."

There was no warmth in the man's expression when he responded to Diego's apology, "The Comandante is taking a personal interest in the case. He intends to prove she was involved with Fuentes and his organization."

"Why does he have it in for her?" Diego asked.

"Because she is frequently at the centre of policía investigations and she is difficult to deal with."

"Impertinent and defiant, that's our Jessica." Thinking about all the crap that was being posted on social media, Diego's face sagged.

Ramirez maintained his stone-faced countenance. "Comandante Camara deserves respect."

Diego pulled in a long calming breath, curbing an angry retort. In his opinion the man did not automatically deserve respect solely because he wore a hat with a pile of gold braid and as far as Diego could see, Camara had done nothing to earn respect.

The sergeant held up his hand, and motioned zip-it with his thumb and forefinger. He lifted his phone off the table and powered it down. He pointed at Diego, indicating he should do the same.

Perplexed Diego complied, then asked, "What's going on? Why did you want me to turn off my phone?"

"Because of something Cervera told me," Ramirez answered, then explained the possibility of someone listening to their conversations via commonly downloaded apps.

"That's very disturbing," Diego said, staring suspiciously at the innocuous looking device.

"Si, very disturbing," Ramirez placed his arms on the table and tipped a tight smile at Diego. "I have concerns and I needed to be convincing."

"Well you certainly had me going," Diego huffed. "The locals know the Comandante is an unscrupulous buffoon. He's probably the one that was on Fuentes payroll and wants to deflect the suspicion onto Jessica."

"It's possible," Ramirez conceded. "That's why I am being very careful."

"So, if this conversation was just an act does that mean you believe Jessica?"

"Mostly," Ramirez said. "I can't help being suspicious of everyone when the cartel is involved. There is a lot of money to be made working with them." Again, he held up his hand, "Si, si. I know you believe Jessica is innocent but I have to maintain my objectivity while we investigate this incident."

"Well, at least the Comandante can't blame her for Fuentes death."

"What's that supposed to mean?" Ramirez asked, his stony expression had returned.

"I meant that I'm relieved that you, a police sergeant, killed him," Diego replied. "There is no way the Comandante can hold her responsible for that."

Ramirez grunted. "Verdad."

Chapter 39

May 14th Cancun

"So, to recap." Toledo rested his elbows on the table, "Fuentes is dead. The war between his lieutenant Ventura Rodriguez and his brother Matías to be the next drug lord has started. And we haven't stopped the ATM scammers." Toledo leaned back in his chair. His hands flopped open on either side, inviting anyone to refute his terse summation.

"Si. That about covers it," Ramirez agreed. "We've solved nothing."

"As far as we know the Romanian gang has moved operations, but is still in business." Cervera reached for the bottle of wine, topping up his wife's glass before refilling his own. "All we have done is cut off one of the heads of the Hydra."

"Hydra?" Toledo asked. "What's that?"

"A mythical Greek creature. When you cut off one head and another one replaces it."

"*Maldito*," Toledo muttered. "Lo siento, *Doña* Beatriz for my language."

She smiled, dismissing his apology, "*No hay problema*, Dante. You know my Marco can be very colourful with his words."

Ramirez' attention briefly wandered from the conversation about cartels, and cursing, and mythical creatures. He inhaled the lingering aromas that attested to Beatriz' love of creating delicious meals for family and friends.

Ramirez missed that. Neither he nor Alexis were interested in cooking due in equal parts to their *loco* shift schedules and their lazy approach to good nutrition. They lived on take-out meals from the neighbourhood taquerias; filling and inexpensive but high on fat and carbohydrates. At some point their eating habits would catch up with them. They could develop diabetes, or heart problems, or perhaps have a stroke. Or either one could be killed on the job, so there really was no point in worrying about the what-ifs.

"*Doña Beatriz, muchas gracias por la deliciosa comida*," Ramirez interjected. "Muy rica." He kissed the ends of his fingers-tips in a gesture reminiscent of a European gentleman, complimenting the chef.

"My pleasure Felipe," Beatriz said, a pleased smile enveloping her round face.

"Do we have a multi-headed creature like the Hydra?" Toledo asked, pulling Ramirez' attention back to the discussion.

"We?" Cervera queried. He looked around the table and pointed at each person as if he was checking everyone had just one head. "No," He said, "I don't think *we* do."

"I meant the Mayan culture. Do we have a Hydra look-alike?" Toledo said, "Perdón," He added stifling a burp. "*La comida estuvo deliciosa*."

"I don't know anything about Mayan mythology. We didn't learn about our culture at school," Cervera shrugged. "I only know stuff that I occasionally pick up from the old folks."

"Si, we do," Alexis answered.

"We do?" Asked Toledo. "Cool."

Ramirez could see her face pink up with embarrassment when four pairs of eyes turned to her with interested surprise.

"Go ahead professor," He teased. His partner was self-conscious of her intelligence. Alexis didn't want give the impression she was a know-it-all, an expert, but damn the woman was smart. She was the one that figured out how to immediately help

Jessica, rather than let the situation drag on. Alexis should be employed at a job where she could be promoted, not stuck forever as a constable in the municipal police force.

"One head represents a crocodile and the other one a serpent," Alexis said. "The creature is thought to be the goddess who brings the rain and births the sun every morning. That's all I know," She finished lamely. Ramirez tried to catch her eye, to give her a supportive wink but she seemed fascinated by her glass of wine.

"Huh, that really interesting," Toledo remarked, then shifted his attention to Ramirez. "What's happening with your suspensions?" He asked.

"The Comandante has decided that we can return to work," Ramirez answered. "He hasn't said that we are completely exonerated but at least we are back working."

"And getting paid again," Alexis muttered.

"Si, there's that," Agreed Ramirez. With both of them being employed by the municipally even just five days of unpaid suspension was financially difficult.

Toledo set his glass of Don Julio on the table. "What about Jessica Sanderson? Does he still suspect her of being involved with Fuentes?"

"He's backed off investigating her as well," Ramirez said. "There wasn't any evidence to support his suspicions, and she has a lot of influential friends on the island. He can't push the issue any further."

"Changing the subject," Cervera said, "You realize we look like a bunch of incompetent goofballs. Right?"

Toledo studied his partner, "Why?" He sounded offended.

"This is the one time that mutt, Sparky, screwed up. He didn't solve the crime so we have no one to arrest," Cervera guffawed loudly.

The others sputtered with laughter. Ramirez thought it was a ridiculous statement, but so near to the truth it really was hilarious.

"Maybe it's a good thing, otherwise if Sparky keeps solving our crimes, we'd have to change our name to the Paw Patrol," Toledo said, slapping the table as he laughed at his own joke.

"Exactly!" Agreed Cervera. "But don't repeat that at the station or we'll never hear the end of it."

"Woof!" Toledo taunted.

Cervera pointed at his partner. "I mean it Dante, don't repeat it."

"*Patrulla de la Pata*," Toledo grinned wickedly.

~

"Damn it, Dante," Cervera whispered harshly. He stopped, checked for eavesdroppers, then continued berating his partner. "I told you not to mention your stupid joke to anyone at the station."

"Marco, chill out. I just got here," Toledo said, setting his container of hot coffee on his desk. He held out a second coffee to Cervera. The offering was ignored, so Toledo set the beverage on his desk. "What's going on?"

"I arrived at work this morning, and guess what's sitting on my desk?"

"No clue."

"An internet advertisement for that ... *movie* ... you mentioned last night," He said through gritted teeth.

"Paw Patrol?"

"Shhh. Be quiet," Cervera hissed.

"Marco, I didn't say anything," Toledo protested. "I was only ribbing you."

An older detective ambled towards their desks. He carefully set down two large dog biscuits, one beside each cup. "You're such good boys. Here's a treat." His rumbling laughter trailed in his footsteps.

Toledo and Cervera both said at the same time. "Ramirez."

Cervera snatched up his phone and pounded at the contact button for Ramirez. "I'll rip off his *huevos*," He said. The side of his right foot repeatedly wacked against the leg of the desk while he waited for the sergeant to answer.

"Bueno," Ramirez said.

"Ja. Ja. Really funny, *pendejo*," Cervera barked.

"Cervera?" Ramirez asked. "Is that you?"

"Of course, it is. Did you really think you'd get away with it?"

"Get away with what?" There was no laughter in his voice. "What are you talking about?" He sounded genuinely perplexed.

Whispering harshly into the phone Cervera said, "Paw Patrol, you spread that around our unit. Everyone is laughing at us."

"No. Not me," Ramirez retorted. "And before you ask, not Alexis either."

"You're lying," Cervera snapped. "That was an inside joke among friends. Now you've made Toledo and I look like idiots."

"We've worked a lot of the same cases. It would make us look ridiculous too. We didn't do it."

Cervera went silent as he considered another possibility. "Did you turn off your phones last night when we had dinner?" He probed.

"I didn't. Did you?"

"No." Cervera pulled in a breath.

"Okay, I'm sorry I jumped on you," Cervera said,

"Call me back when you figure it out. Si?" Ramirez hesitantly asked as if he was thinking along the same lines.

Had someone tapped their phones?

"Claro. Hasta luego." Cervera abruptly disconnected, and cut a look at Toledo. "How about we grab a few rays on the roof before we get stuck working these files?" He said, picking up the coffee that Toledo had earlier offered him.

He flipped the two dog biscuits into his garbage can.

Chapter 40

May 19th Isla Mujeres

"Jesus H. Christ. That hurt." Jessica muttered.

The little cart had slammed into yet another wide wound slashed across the pavement of the perimeter road. In the pre-dawn light, it was difficult to see all the *topes*, pavement breaks, and potholes. Her bruises were fading but her ribs were still sore and she had the remnants of the two shiners.

"You okay, little man?" She glanced down at Sparky.

Sparky turned and met her eyes. His tail flapped twice. His leash was tightly secure around the steering column and he was standing firmly on the floor, not dangling precariously over the open edge of the vehicle.

"What a raggedy mess, you are," Jessica continued talking to her pooch. "Your auntie Yasmin tried her best but you look like hell."

Yasmin had, in several areas, been forced to clip close to his skin to remove the gluey duct tape.

"It'll grow back and you will be as handsome as ever." Not willing to take a hand off the steering wheel to reassure him with a pat, she just smiled sadly. *Poor little guy, he's had so much trauma this year*.

Slowing to cross another cut in the pavement she grumbled aloud, "I wish the municipal and water folks would get their act together and finish this damn project." Upgraded water and sewer services were slowly being installed for the numerous new and existing homes on both sides of the island. In the meantime, many drivers dodged around the wide cuts across the pavement; weaving back and forth across the road at all hours of the day or night.

"Finally," She said as they avoided the last pothole and stopped in front of a thick rope draped across the entrance to the park. She shut off the engine, switched off the headlights and undid Sparky's leash, letting him run freely. He wouldn't wander. He knew the routine.

Ignoring the *Cerrado* sign Jessica ducked under the rope and said good morning to the night watchman, calling him by name and asking if he had had a quiet night. She handed him the entrance fee. For a few pesos anyone could walk to the end of the island and watch the sunrise, while standing beside the ruins of a Mayan watchtower. It was, in her mind, a spiritual experience.

The watchman smiled tiredly, and replied, "Si, gracias, Jessica. Todo bien."

"Solo treinta minutos mas," She said. In thirty minutes, he could drag his tired ass home and hopefully get a good rest before his next shift.

"Si. Hasta luego," He responded sleepily, covering a big yawn with his fist.

She waved goodbye and whistled at Sparky to hurry up.

Sparky was not going to be rushed. This was the most important part of his walk. He carefully sniffed his way along the path, checking for the *pee news* left by other dogs. She grinned at his mulishness and continued walking along the crumbling and uneven footpath towards the most easterly location in Mexico, Punta Sur.

The two dozen or so modern metal statues that were installed in 2001, had recently been removed. Many had become safety hazards through a combination of rust, corrosion, no maintenance, or the insistence of visitors that they should climb the structures to take a perfect vacation souvenir photo. The park looked empty as if something was missing, but at the same time she liked the more natural appearance of the area. In time the vegetation would cover the scars in the earth left by the removal of the crumbling structures.

As she neared the watchtower, she noticed a family grouped around a teenage girl dressed in a gorgeous ball gown. She carried a bouquet of flowers and a bible. A handsome middle-aged priest stood nearby. He was dressed in tailored black pants with a matching shirt, and wore a stylish cream-coloured straw hat.

It was the beginning of a celebration of the young woman's fifteenth birthday and her entrance into womanhood — a quinceañeras. Dressed in their best clothing the beaming parents watched as a videographer recorded the sunrise with their daughter as the centre of their universe.

The juxtaposition of the old Mayan structure and the Catholic priest was fascinating. It would make an interesting photograph, but she didn't know this family and didn't want to intrude.

Skirting around the group Jessica smiled and quietly wished the young woman good luck. Sparky rejoined her as she started down the broken stone stairs to her favourite perch. She hoped her friendly mutt hadn't photobombed the video. He was a pro at mooching pats and compliments from strangers, or lifting a leg and delivering his own edition of the *pee news* for the next dog to read.

She sat on the edge of a disintegrating stair and leaned against the one remaining, well-rotted wooden post. From this location the sun would rise between the two large rocks in front of her, gradually shifting position as it moved further north for the summer and back south again in the winter.

Behind her the sounds of the family group faded away. For them, this was the beginning of a long and joyous celebration starting with a special mass at one of the churches, and ending tomorrow morning with reheated leftovers from the previous night's feast. Perhaps by noon the exhausted family and guests would finally put their heads on pillows and sleep. She had attended three quinceañeras celebrations and envied the certainty, the familiarity of their traditions.

For her, the last few weeks had been tumultuous with murder cropping up once again in her life. She was beginning to feel like a jinx, a magnet for misfortune. Eventually Comandante Camara had stopped pestering her with questions about her alleged relationship with Fuentes. She shuddered; the official whom she distrusted the most had accused her of being the lover of a drug lord. She wasn't certain that Camara actually believed her, but he couldn't prove anything.

Sparky was slowly recovering from their ordeal. He still seemed listless and depressed. He seldom grinned when she spoke silly loving nonsense to him. His tail was down, and tucked. Not once since the attack had she seen his little bristly flag excitedly spinning in what she called helicopter-mode or even rapidly wagging. She was worried about her boy.

Diego had tried to reassure her pooch; *even superheroes don't win every battle against the forces of evil*. She could see Sparky didn't believe him. He seemed to think his job was to protect her, at all cost.

Then there was Ryan Whitecross. He has once again slunk off the island, like a street dog kicked once too often. Diego and Pedro had confessed that after the break-in at her house they had chatted with Whitecross. Diego admitted that maybe, just maybe, they had rattled him a bit.

A shoe scraping the pathway behind her caused Jessica to leap to her feet and spin around. Her hands were set, ready to defend herself. A man lifted a hand in embarrassed acknowledgement.

"I'm really sorry, I didn't mean to startle you," He said, a warm smile lighting up his broad face.

"No worries," She replied, curtly. "My dog would have warned me if you were a problem."

The guy was blocking her exit back up the cliff, but if he became a threat, she still had the option of scrambling down a few more stairs and running along the seawall towards Garrafón Park. The pathway was slippery from sea spray, and not the safest route but the events of the last few months had taught her to always have an escape plan.

"He's a cutie. What's his name?"

"Sparky," Jessica answered flatly. She didn't feel sociable and hoped the man would take the hint with her abrupt response. He didn't. He squatted down and extended the back of his hand for Sparky to sniff.

"Hey, little buddy, do you want a scratch?" He asked.

Sparky moved closer and let the new arrival scratch his head then his rump in his favourite spot right at the base of his tail. Jessica chewed her bottom lip, closely watching the man. Her mutt seemed unperturbed by his presence so now she was stuck making polite conversation with a stranger.

"You know this is Sparky, what's your name?"

"Miguel."

"Miguel?" She cocked an eyebrow. He had dark brown hair, pale skin and green eyes flecked with bits of gold. "You don't look or sound like a Miguel."

"You got me," He laughed easily. "My name is Mike Lyons. I'm Canadian, but my family is originally from Ireland." He studied her face as he stuck out his right hand.

"I'm Jessica," She replied ignoring his gesture. She could tell he was curious about the bruises still visible around both of her eyes.

"You should have seen the other guy," She quipped. Watching his expression change to surprised amusement, she relented and shook his outstretched hand.

"Mucho gusto, Mike Lyons."

El Fin

About the author

Born in a British Columbia Canada gold mining community that is now essentially a ghost town, Lynda has had a very eclectic working career. Her employment background has included a bank clerk, antique store owner, ambulance attendant, volunteer firefighter, supervisor of the SkyTrain transit control centre, partner in a bed & breakfast, partner in a micro-brewery, and a hotel manager. The adventure and the experience were always far more important than the paycheque.

Writing has always been in the background of her life, starting with travel articles for a local newspaper, an unpublished novel written before her fortieth birthday, and articles for an American safety magazine.

When she and her husband, Lawrie Lock, retired to Isla Mujeres, Mexico in 2008, they started a weekly blog, Notes from Paradise - Isla Mujeres, to keep friends and family up to date on their newest adventure.

Needing something more to keep her active mind occupied, Lynda and island friend, Diego Medina, self-published a bi-lingual book for children, The Adventures of Thomas the Cat / Las Aventuras de Tómas el Gato. The book won Silver at the 2016 International Latino Book Awards for best bi-lingual picture book for children.

Be the first to know when Lynda's next book is available! Follow her on any of her social media links to get an alert whenever she has a new release, pre-order, or discount!

Wordpress Isla Mujeres Mystery
Facebook Lynda L Lock
Twitter Isla Mysteries
Instagram Isla Mysteries
Amazon Lynda L Lock
Bookbub Lynda L Lock
Goodreads Lynda L Lock

The legal stuff

The characters and events in this book are purely fictional except the following:

Jessica Sanderson is a product of my imagination but like me, she was born in BC Canada. She shares my off-beat sense of humour and a love of critters.

Carlos Mendoza is in many ways my husband Lawrie Lock. He shares his good sense of humour, the love of dancing, plus the appreciation of Rolex watches and expensive cars. Lawrie and his three life-long buddies managed to get into a few interesting situations when they were younger. Lawrie occasionally used the politically incorrect quips, including a *pirate's delight*, included in *Terror Isla*.

Yasmin Medina is completely fictitious, but she is tall with curly hair similar to my friend Yazmin Aguirre.

The *Loco Lobo Restaurant* is also fictitious, it is not based on any particular location or restaurant.

Terror Isla
Published by Lynda L. Lock

Print Copy: ISBN 978 1 775 3788 3 9
Electronic Book: ISBN 978 1 775 3788 2 2

Hola amigos y amigas

Pardon my lack of Spanish. I keep trying to learn, but every night while I am sleeping the words leak out of my brain and onto the pillow.

In a perfect world I would have written this story in Spanish or in this case Isla-Spanish which is a colourful mix of local expressions and a bit of Mayan tossed in for added flavour.

However, most of my readers are English speaking. So, for the purpose of this story the local folks are fluent in both Spanish and English, especially the cuss words.

I chose to *italicise* only a few of the less familiar Spanish expressions. For my American fans you will probably notice I spell some words differently. The British-Canadian spelling that I grew up with is what I use.

Like every self-published writer, I rely heavily on recommendations and reviews to sell my books. If you enjoyed reading any of my *Isla Mujeres Mystery* novels please leave a review on Amazon, Goodreads, Kobo, B&N Nook, iTunes, Bookbub, Smashwords, Facebook or Twitter.

If you come across an annoying blunder please email me at: lock.lynda@gmail.com and I will make it disappear.

Like this book? Please try the others!

Buy all 4 books with one click

Acknowledgements

Writing is a solitary obsession with hours spent creating, considering, and correcting.

However, I have had assistance from some amazing people:

- Captain Tony Garcia for the beautiful cover photos for three novels plus the photo of Sparky and me. He is also a valuable source of information about island life.
- You may have guessed by now Tony Garcia and Betsy Snider are good friends. They are owned by several yellow cats, and two dogs. Kitty-Kitty a pale-orange love-bug, is their favourite.
- Carmen Amato, mystery writer and creator of the Emilia Cruz Detective Series re-designed the covers for both *Treasure Isla* and *Trouble Isla*.
- Our good friends Diego Medina and Jeff McGahee patiently tweaked the cover for *Tormenta Isla* until I was happy with the results. Diego Medina created the covers for Temptation Isla and Terror Isla from some of my photos.
- Patricio Yam Dzul and Aida Yolanda Pérez Martín, plus Freddy Medina and Eva Velázquez are cherished friends who are always willing to share their life stories.
- Apache (Isauro Martinez Jr.) another one of my go-to-friends when I am searching for specific information about the island.
- Jerry Bastien for his humorous story about the police and the four young drunks.
- Manuscript and proofreaders include, Rob Goth, Julie Andrews Goth, Sue Lo, Betsy Snider, Denise Hawthorne Thorson, Janice Carlisle Rodgers and Carolina Sanders. I truly appreciate your helpful suggestions and corrections, any and all remaining errors are my responsibility.

There are four other groups of people I would like to thank for their continuing encouragement and support:

- Faithful readers of Notes from Paradise — Isla Mujeres, https://islamystery.com/
- Supporters of my children's book, The Adventures of Thomas the Cat;
- Fans of the Isla Mujeres Mystery series;
- And our island friends, ex-pats and born-here-locals who patiently answered my questions about this and that and everything.

Thank you, thank you, and thank you all!

Love the island? Lend a hand:

Club Pro-Paciente Diabetico Isla Mujeres AC

https://isladiabetesclinic.com/

Diabetes is currently the primary cause of death in Mexico. Many walk-ins are untreated and undiagnosed. The main emphasis of the clinic is diabetes education and distribution of meters. Isleños are taught to use the meters to self-monitor their blood sugar levels.

Helmets for Isla

https://helmetsforisla.weebly.com/

The Isla Mujeres Children's Helmet Campaign was created to address the need to raise awareness about the importance of wearing a helmet and to supply helmets to children in need. The campaign seeks to provide all elementary aged children with helmets.

Helping Animals Living Overseas

https://www.helpinganimalslivingoverseas.org/

Helping Animals Living Overseas (HALO) is a registered not-for-profit society. The Isla Mujeres animal hospital has gas anesthesia, an x-ray machine, and two blood chemistry analyzers. They offer free spay & neuter surgeries and help re-home many dogs and cats. Play with the kittens, walk a recovering dog, or foster an animal.

Isla Animals

http://islaanimals.org/about-isla-aminals/

The Isla Animals volunteer team has instigated a system of trap, sterilize and release of stray animals, or adoption where possible. Isla Animals has organized and sponsored at least two spay and neuter campaigns each year. The rescue continues to offer free spay & neuter surgeries two days a week and free or low-cost medicines for dogs and cats.

Isla Kids – Give a Little! Help a Lot!

https://islakids.org/

The mission of Isla Kids is to assist needy children and families. Their current project is focused on supporting and assisting the children of Casa Hogar in Rancho Viejo, a poorer section of the municipality of Isla Mujeres located on the mainland. All kids need is a little help, a little hope and someone who believes in them.

Isla Mujeres Cats Need Help

https://www.facebook.com/islamujerescatsneedhelp/

Josefina Rodriguez Martinez has about fifty cats at her home and goes twice a day to feed strays. She also assists with trapping the hundreds of feral cats on the island so that they can be spayed or neutered.

Isla Scholarship Program

https://www.islascholarships.com/about-the-scholarship-program

The program began in 2005 with a handful of high school students and six sponsors. As high school students graduated and wanted to continue their education, teams of sponsors were formed to meet the increased expenses. You can invest in Isla's future by helping a student.

Little Yellow School House -

http://littleyellowschoolhouse.org/

The Little Yellow School House on Isla Mujeres began with one room, six students and a really big dream. Their aim is to educate local children who have physical, emotional, or learning disabilities. The funds raised at various events during the annual Island Time Music Festival are donated to the Little Yellow School House. It's a win-win situation for everyone.

Ruben's Three Kings Day

http://rubensthreekingsday.org/

Known as Día de Los Reyes, in Mexico, it is celebrated on January 6th. This is the day that children receive their seasonal gifts. For several years Ruben Chavez has hosted the event at his restaurant in Centro Isla Mujeres. There are refreshments for the children and families, hampers for families in need and of toys for the kids thanks to many generous donations!

The Ron Brown Scholarship Fund

http://ronbrownscholarshipfund.org/

The goal of the RBSF is to provide financial assistance to promising, dedicated students in order to further their education and enable them to improve their lifestyle. This opportunity will not only benefit the students, but also their families and in turn, the whole community.

Yucatan Education Project

https://yucataneducationproject.org/

Yearly about 300 children start high school but only 60 finish. Higher quality local jobs are taken by residents of Cancun. Approximately 7000 people come daily from Cancun to work on the Isla. On-island education will be available for 300 young men and women in the following areas: Hotel management, languages, computer science, gastronomy, and tourism.

Zapatos Para Los Niños Shoes for Children - Mexico

https://www.shoesforchildrenmx.com/

Zapatos Para Los Niños (Shoes for the Children) was started by Greg and Natalie Snider from Oregon. Since 2015 Don and Brenda Gentry have continued the mission. In 2019 they more than doubled their original goal of 500 pairs by providing 1029 pairs of shoes to needy children.

For readers who are a little Spanish-challenged

Bruja del Mar – Literally witch of the sea, Sea Witch
Carina – urban slang for a funny, gorgeous, and amazing girlfriend
Casita – small house
Casa – house
Chucka-chucka – humorous Mayan euphemism for sex
Cómo está? – How are you?
Con permiso – to move around or past a person
Don or Doña – respectful title used with the person's first name
Hermano – brother, or any male who is like a brother
Hermana – sister, or any female who is like a sister
Hijo de la chingada – crude curse, son of a bitch
Hola – hi or hello
Hombre – man
La Trigueña – The young woman Mundaca loved
Loco Lobo – Crazy Wolf, also El Loco Lobo but one of our Mexican friends said Loco Lobo sounded better
Maldito – darn, damn
Mama – mom   Mami – mommy
Mande? – The person didn't hear you.
Más o menos – more or less
Mi amor – my love
Mierda – swear word, shit
Mordidita – bribe, literally a little bite
Motos – motor scooters, motor bikes
Niña(s) – girl or girls
Niño(s) – boy or boys, can also mean children
Papa – dad   Papi – daddy
Pendejo – swear word
Que pasa – what's happening
Que pasó – what happened
Pícaro – horndog, randy male
Rapido – rapid, fast
Tia – auntie, or an older female who is like an aunt
Tio – uncle, or an older male who is like an uncle
Topes – speed bumps

Sparky and his writer

Made in the USA
Middletown, DE
17 September 2019